PEOPLE SKINS

VOL. II

DARK, STRANGE AND
FANTASTIC STORIES

MORGAN DELANEY

Copyright © 2022 by Morgan Delaney.

This is a work of fiction. I made everything up. Any similarity between the characters and situations within its pages and places or persons, living or dead, is unintentional and co-incidental.

All rights reserved. No part of this publication may be reproduced, distributed or transmitted in any form or by any means, including photocopying, recording, or other electronic or mechanical methods, without the prior written permission of the publisher, except in the case of brief quotations embodied in critical reviews and certain other noncommercial uses permitted by copyright law. For permission requests, write to the contact email address below.

Published by Morgan Delaney

Contact: morgan@morgandelaney.info

www.morgandelaney.info

Edited by Julian Barr

Cover design by MiblArt

People Skins Volume 2 / Morgan Delaney. —1st edition 2022

Ebook ISBN 978-3-98566-009-4

Audiobook ISBN 978-3-98566-011-7

Print ISBN 978-3-98566-010-0

Contents

Beauty is skin deep.
Cut deeper.

People Skins, Volume 0: Hidden Cuts features 5 more tales of off-beat fantasy and surreal horror—but only for subscribers:
a sheriff finds ice-cold dread in the middle of a red-hot desert;
Ireland's miracle of moving religious statues becomes a nightmare;
Rose, Henry, and Reg are friends, lovers, and playing a deadly game;
Maria doesn't believe a ghost haunts the phone box. But she will;
a fugitive pirate ship encounters a wreck with a mind of its own.

Join me to get your *Hidden Cuts now!*
(https://morgandelaney.info/newsletter/)

For Nadine,
who makes my heart feel like it might burst.

Film Material

This supernatural ghost story is for the film fans.
I mention Peter Greenaway and his film, The Falls, *which are real.*
The cinema everything takes place in, Das Panische Lichtspielhaus,
is based on two real Berlin cinemas (Moviemento in Neukölln and
Sputnik in Kreuzberg).
The goat statue exists.
But as for the rest?
Well, I'd love to see a skin-flick directed by Peter Greenaway, if there
was one.
Although not if it meant bumping into Eberhardt Vesper, the late
cinema owner...

"Ihr scheiß Wichser! Verdammte Scheißwichser!"

Cal didn't speak German, but he knew the guy wasn't happy. The old punk—or junkie?—wore a brown flat cap. He had straggly nicotine-yellow hair and wore a sleeveless vest which might once have been purple. His black boots, laced up to the knees, had burst around the toes. The sweet smell as Cal passed him could have been from the man's thick woollen socks or the weed on his breath. He ranted at the traffic light, waiting for it to turn green. Cal wished he had the courage to take a photo. His camera hung from his neck, but he didn't want to get involved. Couldn't afford another delay.

He'd taken the wrong U-Bahn. When he'd made it back to Schönleinstraße, he'd taken the wrong exit and walked the wrong way, landing at Hermannplatz before noticing.

Friday evening. The streets buzzed with a mix of early partiers and late shoppers. They seethed past, laughing over the heavy traffic on Kottbusser Damm. It was his first time in Berlin and he was late. He felt homesick when he heard someone talking English, despite their Spanish accent.

There was enough daylight left to take a quick shot of the cinema when he found it. He'd have to come back in the morning. The exterior was coated in flyers and film posters. Grainy with exhaust fumes. A nearby park with a life-size statue of a goat told him he'd arrived. The goat gleamed in the warm drizzle which started falling. He hurried inside, following an arrow to the stairs.

The notorious cinema, *Das Panische Lichtspielhaus,* was on the top floor of the five-storey building.

Five decades of underground cinema history in two auditoriums.

One haunting.

No lift.

Cal jogged up the stairs, cursing everyone who raved about the wonderful high ceilings of Berlin apartments and buildings when he had told them about his trip. He was out of breath by the second floor, built for films, not Instagram. And he was late. He hated it when people came in late to a film and tonight wasn't merely a film. It was an event.

His camera punched him in the stomach with every step, and the sting of fresh paint burned his nostrils. He slowed to a walk, pulling himself up by the bannisters. Fluorescent lighting hummed. He kept going, past heavy steel doors, two per floor, each with an ornate spyhole surrounded with notices, all dense with German text.

He'd come all this way for nothing. They'd laugh at him when he arrived at the top. *You're* the reviewer? Amazed that he couldn't make it on time. He kept going, ignoring the damp patches growing under his armpits, turning his orange t-shirt umber. He sucked air through his mouth, coating his throat with the medicinal smell of oil paint. If nothing else, he could get a photo of the foyer, at least. Maybe he'd bump into a famous director. No chance of Greenaway himself, who'd disowned the film. But maybe he'd bump into Buttgereit, who was a Berliner. He was bound to be there tonight.

Or if some random guy was hanging around, he could pretend it was the reclusive Eberhardt Jr. Nobody would know.

He could get a drink and maybe sneak in later. Or if they left him alone, sneak into the haunted auditorium, which was what he really wanted. Cal even had an extra fifty Euro tucked into his pocket, if that was what it took.

Mick would kill him if he messed this up. He'd never give him another assignment.

Mick lived for films and had a network of—no judgement—weirdos, who kept him informed for his podcast. Mick had arranged the plane ticket and seen Cal off at the airport before anyone else even heard the rumour that the lost Peter Greenaway film might have re-surfaced. And it was Mick who broke the news that not only was the film back, but was being shown in the *Das Panische Lichtspielhaus*, where it had had its premiere.

Its first and only showing.

Mick's problem was that the cinema was still run by the Vespers. Eberhardt Junior had taken over the business after his father's death, and they were as sneaky—and as good at marketing—as Mick. Mick couldn't risk his reputation in case this was just the latest in a long line of publicity stunts.

Hence Cal, who didn't mind. Even if it was a publicity stunt, it was a legitimate assignment. See the film, get a snap of the ghost. If he nailed it, he'd get more. If he couldn't, he'd be back at the cafe, stuck behind the counter wrapping take-away orders, because his boss said he gave customers the creeps.

Through the paint, he smelled buttery popcorn. He felt sick by the time he made it to the top floor, and his legs were going to ache the next day. Two vintage floor lamps replaced the fluorescent lighting, and burgundy walls replaced the metal doors. The railing was painted gold, as were the stucco on the ceiling and the cherubs which bloomed everywhere. They hung from the ceiling, swarming around the bulbless light fittings, peeped from the corners, half-hid behind the lamps. A firing-line row of six hung on the wall in front of him. He barely avoided walking into one that lurked at the top of the steps. Their golden skin was cracked, their featureless eyes stared at hordes of cinema-goers that Cal couldn't see. He raised his camera.

"No pictures!" The guy suddenly blocking Cal's way could have been the punk/junkie's more successful brother. Long grey hair swayed loosely about his gaunt head, but he wore clean jeans and a neat black t-shirt. By Berlin standards, he was practically natty. He sized Cal up. "You're late," he said. German with a clipped American accent.

"*The Tables?*" said Cal.

"*Ja,*" said the man, which sounded like a drawled American, "yah." He stood behind a school table covered with a thick red velvet cloth. The same material hung over the walls of the foyer behind him. Pink tickets coiled on the table beside a blue metal cash box. Cal handed over ten Euro in exchange for a ticket, the thick paper furry between his fingers.

"Drink?" said the man, ushering Cal past him. He stood close; the doorway was narrow. In the foyer, three plush couches ran the length of the walls, each with its own small marble table. A large golden "1" indicated the main auditorium, but the corridor was roped off, the door in darkness.

Auditorium One was haunted.

A "2" led to the smaller auditorium, which is where Greenaway's *The Tables* was being shown.

Between them was the refreshment stand. A single beer tap and a small chest freezer for ice cream. Butter had glazed the popcorn machine's window brown and shelves behind it held neat rows of chocolates and sweets. It was all a lot smaller than Cal had expected. The cinema smelled like cigarettes and dust.

He ordered a beer to wash the paint out of his throat, and some Skittles for something to fidget with in case he had to sit next to someone. The man took his time pouring the beer, and they faced each other silently. Cal realised the man must be Eberhardt Jr and he couldn't think of a single thing to say. So he ordered an ice cream, hoping that was small talk enough.

For his part, the man was trying not to grin. He tossed his hair back to disguise the twitch in his cheek.

Cal would ask about the haunted auditorium later.

The one where the first Eberhardt Vesper had hanged himself.

During the original premiere of *The Tables*.

His corpse dangling in the flickering light until the credits had rolled off the screen.

———

The man, who must have been Eberhardt Jr, opened the first of the two sets of double doors that led to the film. He pointed to Cal's camera and waggled a shrivelled finger before Cal disappeared into the dark. He took a moment to let his eyes adjust, listening for the sound of the film. He'd made it. His stomach unknotted as he tucked the Skittles into his pocket and pushed open the inner doors.

Noise burst on him as he entered right below the enormous screen. Orange and pink swirls tumbled. The roar was like the ocean as the swirls toppled over each other, threatening to pour out, wash him away. There were just a few dozen seats, dimly lit by the reflected colours of the screen. Half a dozen rows with ten seats each. Empty as far as he could see. No need to worry about having to sit next to anybody, but the light was dizzying and the noise deafening. A set of steps on the far side of the auditorium led to the back rows. He ducked his head and scurried over to them.

He bumped into a figure at the bottom of the steps. A tall man with his hand out. A ticket man, then. Cal gave him his ticket, his head still bowed to avoid obstructing the screen.

The Ticketman was thin and so tall that Cal couldn't see his face. He wore all black, even his gloves, which might have looked classy, but were hardly practical. Cal's pink ticket seemed to hover in the darkness until he took it back and the figure let him pass.

Cal hurried towards the second row from the back. Middle seat. He counted the steps, feeling with his toes for the next one in the dark. He heard his own breath and the ticking of the film reel. Lost count of the steps. Started counting again and reached fifteen before he bumped into someone. The Ticketman again. Light seeped out of the screen and he excused himself, hoping to gain his seat before it faded. The film roared, and the Ticketman followed him. There was enough light now to see the back wall and the seats. Cal slipped into his row and dropped into the middle seat as the dawn arrived on screen and the camera swooped.

A long shot of the Roman Colosseum from above. The arena wall was a dead eye, the pupil white and twitching. The camera plunged to the centre, and the twitching resolved into crowds, shouting, running, dancing. All naked. Cheering or jeering at two central characters. The infamous opening scene: Caligula with his horse. Unmistakable Greenaway.

Cal grinned, then remembered he hadn't brought a notebook or anything. He looked around and was disgusted to note someone sitting right in front of him. The auditorium was now bathed in light and Cal saw that, although the auditorium was almost empty, there were a few heads here and there and one couple near the front, to the right. He must have passed them on his way up the stairs, but the Ticketman had had his full attention. If the film turned out to be just a publicity stunt for the cinema, then it hadn't worked.

The guy in front of Cal had thick curly hair and a very round head. Luckily, he sat slumped in his seat so it wasn't in the way.

Around him, the sound of the shouting on screen crowd filled the room. It grew and grew. Cal winced and sank in his seat to get away from it. There was a hissing sound, too, under the ticking of the projector. The print may have been damaged before Vesper found it again. Cal put his feet up on his seat, then noticed the Ticketman in the aisle. He leant against the wall near Cal's row. Cal put his feet back on the floor, where they glued themselves to the sticky carpet.

He sipped his beer and watched the film. He'd have to remember everything. Shook his head to dislodge the hissing and ticking. It pushed inside his head like rising air pressure on a plane.

It was an early film. Having only made shorts up to that point, Greenaway jumped at the chance, when Penthouse offered to fund his first feature. It was the Golden Age of Porn, and they wanted something dirty and epic. Greenaway, by all accounts, gave it to them. He based the story on the astrological writings of Thrasyllus.

In real life, Thrasyllus died before Caligula ascended the throne. In Greenaway's retelling, he survived to see his prediction that Caligula would become emperor come true. The twist was that it was well-meaning Thrasyllus who drove Caligula insane.

Thrasyllus had previously advised Tiberius, Caligula's father, and soon had Caligula under his sway, too. A gifted astrologer, Thrasyllus created two sets of charts, or tables. One set of forty-six tables was purely astrological. The other forty-six foretold of catastrophes. Penthouse wanted 'mind-blowing orgies' and Greenaway provided them, on the premise that Thrasyllus convinced the prudish young Caligula to arrange them to change the future.

By ensuring that key figures are, or are not born, the disasters can be avoided. The film ended with Thrasyllus describing the forty-sixth and worst catastrophe. The distraught Caligula asked how they would avert it and when Thrasyllus told him it could not be done, it was a consequence of their meddling, the jaded Emperor lost his mind. This catastrophe turns out to be the Violent Unknown Event of Greenaway's follow-up, *The Falls*. Without *The Tables*, therefore, there was no way to understand what Greenaway was attempting to do with the later film.

According to Mick, anyway.

Cal's eyes were sore. The screen was too big and Greenaway had packed it with too much information. It was like watching all the case studies from *The Falls* simultaneously. He slouched lower in his seat, exhausted and feeling sorry for the people sitting near the front. And he had lost track of the plot already. One thing was for certain though: there was an absolutely staggering amount of flesh and fucking on screen.

He was grateful for a respite, while Thrasyllus deciphered the prophecy of a famine caused when a king, insulted by a ribald song which mentioned him, refused to allow his subjects to tend their harvest as punishment. Thrasyllus worked backwards through the king's lineage until he found a Roman soldier in it and advised Caligula that the man would make a perfect eunuch. The soldier was castrated and his stiffened prick was passed around to anyone who wanted it during the subsequent orgy.

Penthouse mightn't have liked that bit, but it didn't bother anyone in the audience. Cal had expected everyone to wince or groan, but there was no response. He could almost believe he was the only person here. Sitting by himself with cardboard cut-outs to fill out the audience.

Something was still hissing. It ebbed when Thrasyllus worked on his astrology and predictions, waxed during every orgy, as the actors rubbed themselves against each other, trying to scratch and mortify their sinful flesh. But it was in the auditorium, too. The agonised hiss of someone expelling their breath even as they held their finger over a candle-flame. Nobody reacted to it.

The Ticketman stood, a black shadow against the wall. Was it Vesper hissing at Cal? In the darkness, the figure was just shoulders. It looked like someone had hung a black tunic on the wall. Cal looked up for the beam of light that carried the film from the projector to the screen.

He couldn't find it, but noticed that he wasn't in the second last row, after all. There were several rows behind him, with someone sitting directly behind him.

Cal's scalp itched. He hated being watched. And, having been sure there was no one behind him, he felt cheated. There didn't even seem to be a projector in the back wall, so it was likely just a DVD. He'd thought he was getting a real *film* film. The hissing wasn't the celluloid being fed into the machine, just something on the soundtrack to fool him. And the cinema was all but empty. So much for the Vesper's famous publicity stunts. He'd wasted all this time and money. It was barely a proper cinema at all.

He turned back to the screen, hunching down lower still in his seat.

At least the film was interesting, if not enjoyable.

———

Eberhardt Vesper had set up *Das Panische Lichtspielhaus* in the 1970s, when he was already an old man. He obsessed over films and had spent most of his life attempting to break into film-making.

Realising he never would, he set up the cinema to get the films to come to him. And they did. From Kenneth Anger to Andy Warhol, they flocked to his *Lichtspielhaus*.

Then, already having doubts about the film, Penthouse had decided to hold the world premiere of *The Tables* in the relatively small main auditorium, which was only large enough to hold a "select audience."

It wasn't until after the lights had come back on that Vesper's body was discovered, suspended in the tunnel of light from the projector.

It was the last straw. The film's production had been beset by numerous technical difficulties already, and the suicide spelled the end. Penthouse had produced the film to cash in on the wave of hardcore sex successes throughout the 1970s. They had been willing to give an unknown English director a chance, to try and make something with a veneer of class.

But they had a Plan B, too, and a simpler script for a Caligula story already commissioned. They didn't need more negative publicity.

The Tables disappeared.

———

The entire film was hands and bellies and mouths and tits and dicks. And moustaches. Sometimes they really were moustaches and sometimes they were pubic hair. Brought up on clean-shaven porn, Cal found it upsetting. He dreaded every close-up. It added to his disorientation, especially when he guessed wrong.

That was pubic hair.

That was a moustache. Because that was a tongue snaking out, not an organ prolapsing (a genuine concern considering how vigorous the action was).

He focused on the head in front of him instead. The hair was black, curly. Thick and greasy. It didn't move.

Cal's head itched. The guy behind him must still be watching him. Cal shifted position to let the guy know he was still alive

In case that was what he was wondering.

On the screen, the orgy moved into the fresh air and the hairs on the head in front of him were lit up. They didn't move at all. Not even when Cal leaned forward and blew on them.

He wanted to go, but Ticketman was blocking the aisle. Cal couldn't see if he was watching the film, he was just a silhouette holding up the wall. He looked two dimensional as he leaned against it. A flicker of light and the head moved, shifted towards him. But the Ticketman's head was not a head at all. It was an eagle's beak without eyes or mouth. A clothes hanger's hook. Cal leaned back in his seat, fumbled with his ice cream.

It had already melted in Cal's hands. The wrapper crinkled as he fought to stop the goo from emptying itself over his camera or trousers. He ended up dropping the whole mess and looked around, in case the Ticketman had seen. But when he looked to where the figure had been, he realised there was no wall there.

The room was bigger than he had thought. There was another block of seating on the far side of the steps that Cal had walked up to get to his seat.

Cal braced himself. He didn't want to draw attention in here, but he had to know. He stood up, waved one sticky hand, then sat back down.

There was no movement from the other seats, so it wasn't a mirror. No wonder he had become lost on his way to the seat. And that explained why the film wasn't being projected over his head: he wasn't in the middle of the room. Which solved two mysteries. But there was something wrong with the other side of the auditorium. The people over there didn't have a screen in front of them. Were they waiting for their film to start?

Cal started sweating. This time, it wasn't his anxiety. It was the heat pouring off the screen, he realised. Another realisation: the people over there weren't in this auditorium. They were in Auditorium One.

But that had been closed and they shouldn't be there. It was the Wrong Auditorium. Anyone in there would be Wrong.

They shouldn't be watching Cal's film, in case it made them want to come over to Cal's auditorium.

There was plenty of room for them. That wasn't the point. These seats are for *us*, not for *you*, he thought. His chest caught.

What if it was no *us* over here, just *me?*

He held his breath, tried to stay as quiet and still as everyone else on his side of the stairs. If he breathed, then the Wrong People in the Wrong Film might realise he was alone, sitting among fake cardboard figures, and come over. Ticketman had kept them at bay, but he had left.

The Wrong People were coming.

A second person sat in the row in front of him. He felt the whisper of a breeze behind him and the itching on the back of his head increased as someone else sat down in the row behind him.

Out of the corner of his eye, he saw a body inflate into place on a seat near the end of his own row.

On screen, Thrasyllus addressed the camera, prophesying disaster again, while the other actors wiped off sweat in the background. The pupils of the actor's eyes twitched and Cal looked away.

Something was moving on the floor in front of him. He remembered his spilled ice cream, but the pale movement came from under the row in front of him and oozed towards his foot. He bent to look closer, glad to get out of the light of the film and the treble rasp of Thrasyllus's monologue. A plastic bag, perhaps. His face was a foot away from it when the thing blinked.

Cal shouted and jerked back. It was thin enough to see through and shiny, like a wormy sheath. It had pale human eyes. They stared up at Cal as he cowered in his seat, hypnotising him as it lifted itself up.

Behind it, the curly head shook and the worm-like thing sank to the ground and seeped back under the chair. There were two people sitting in his row now. Beyond the new figure, Ticketman occupied the very last seat, his legs crossed, blocking any escape. Cal looked around, but there was someone on the other side, too. Far away in the corner. For now.

If he wanted to escape, he had to hurry. They were all watching him. Cal's brain ached from the stare of the person behind him, the ticking sound tapping its way into his skull.

He ducked down, pretending to pick up his ice cream wrapper, then pushed off as hard as he could. He'd keep low to plough through anyone in his way, trample them underfoot if they didn't move.

Something pulled at his neck and he fell. The camera strap was snagged on the edge of his seat. The fall stunned him. His face was at floor level and the carpet was damp with decades of sugary grime under his cheek. Under the seat beside his dazed eyes lay a translucent wormy sheath, folded or rolled up. He looked back at the shadows under the other seat, then at those under the seats in front of him. There were pale eyes under every seat.

Under his seat, his own sheath of rolled up skin waited for him. His hand was on his camera. He had grabbed it automatically to protect it from the fall. He pressed the button, and the room lit up. All the eyes blinked in unison. From under his seat, his roll of skin extended towards him. The eyes looked familiar. It extended towards him and blinked again.

Did I blink? thought Cal.

All he had done was take the white filmy skins' attention off the screen, and earn it for himself.

They blinked. That was the ticking sound he had heard: skin flashing over moist eyes. Sighing and groaning replaced Thrasyllus's voice, and the eyes swivelled back to the screen.

The Ticketman stood up, and the one thing Cal didn't want was to meet him. He scrabbled to his feet and returned to his place.

His scalp itched. He had his ice cream wrapper in one hand and a pale figure sitting in the seat beside him held his other hand. It was nice.

He hummed quietly to himself. Unless he hissed. Forcing the air out slowly, concentrating on breathing and watching the film, so he didn't scream.

He watched the rest of it, read the credits. It was the best thing he'd ever seen, and he knew why Vesper had killed himself on watching it. He understood why all the worms on the screen had been burrowing into each other, scraping their skin off on one another. Losing the dead weight.

His own skin felt tight, like it was coated in candy floss. He dropped his ice cream wrapper again and patted his face. His fingers were too soft to grip the cobweb strands on his eyelashes. If they were still his eyelashes.

The Wrong Auditorium was empty. He could leave that way if he wanted. There was a door into—and out of—it, and no queue waiting to leave.

His name scrolled up the screen. A day player, that was all. It was fine.

The end credits rolled right off the screen. He stood up. Everyone in Auditorium Two stood up. They filed out, waking as the lights came on. Cal slowed to let everyone else pass.

He gave the auditorium a parting glance before he went out the same door he had come in. Both of the auditoriums were now empty. There were no eyes under the seats. And a ticket man hung in the beam of the dying film's light where he belonged.

We Are Here

*As a building manager in Australia, I spent a lot of time keeping Emergency Evacuation Plans up to date in case of fire.
I get it. Australia is hot and burns easily.
In Ireland, if there's a fire, everyone pulls up closer, glad of the chance to dry out.
The point is, when a writing prompt asked me to write a story featuring "some kind of map," I knew exactly what to do.*

I examine the yellowed fire evacuation plan while I wait to visit the ladies' busy restroom at the back of the murky bar. It's dense with extinguishers, hoses, detectors, alarms and exits. If there was a fire, we'd burn in its obstacle course.

Who draws these things? I imagine a failed artist in a faded checked shirt, ripping angry razor-straight lines into soft paper. I look around to get my bearings, then peer again at the plan. "You are here," it says.

That's clever. How did he know?

The line shuffles forward as identical pink-clad blondes leave the restroom, arm-in-arm. I feel eyes on me. Across from our queue, a man leans against the wall. He's a shadow, except for a red puffer jacket, and his greasy black eyes stare through our bellies, like he's imagining our warm full bladders under our clothes. I turn back to the fire plan legend.

"You are here," it says.

That's how he found you, says my brain.

Another evacuation plan hangs pinned between the lifts in the foyer when I get home. I never noticed it before. I guess it's like when you learn a word and then hear it everywhere.

A red dot stands alone in the blank foyer. "You are here." Ice flushes through my veins. Is someone watching me? Updating these stupid maps no one cares about?

In the dark beyond the building's glass doors, a flash of red catches my eye. A worn jacket and black eyes watch me squeeze into the lift before the doors fully open. I jab the button for the eighth floor.

———

I can't hide, the maps are everywhere. "You are here."

Occasionally, I glimpse the greasy-eyed artist. Somebody must be paying him to follow me. Who? And why? I'm not important. Perhaps it's some game that I stumbled into, unlucky, when I saw him that first time.

Trying to drop into sleep, I speculate on the possible rules to distract myself from the draughtsman's pen scratching from my closet.

I see him everywhere, like when you learn a word and… did I say that already?

It must be magic, because the maps always get there—everywhere—first.

"You are here," they announce.

Or it's a trick. One man with body doubles, passing resemblances helped along with black contact lenses, and a wardrobe of worn jackets. But how does he do it, and *why?*

In a random cubicle, in a random restroom in a random town, I realise there can't be a man following me. I'm playing this trick on myself. To prove it, I yank open the door of the next cubicle.

"Is that it?" I demand. "I'm crazy. That's why you're here?"

His black eyes rise over the horizon of his sketchpad. "I'm here," he says. "Because you are." He turns his drawing to show me.

The lettering is so tiny that I have to lean into the tangy sweat of his presence to read it.

Immaculately formed letters fill the cubicle we're in, the second last one from the end.

They say, "We are here."

It Was Always Me

Although I've changed some of the names, this psychological thriller is set "on location" near my University of Sydney haunts, from when I worked there.
I enjoyed living and working in Australia.
If you're thinking of going, just make sure you know who your friends are, eh?

I started going to Maxine's when I was at uni, before things got out of hand. My courses were all on the Camperdown campus in Sydney, but everyone knew Maxine's in Eveleigh, near Redfern, had the best coffee, so I that's where I went. I had three good years at uni, before people starting causing trouble for me. I was out of circulation for a while after that, nearly didn't apply for the job at the nearby Centre, in case it brought back memories. But, you know. I hadn't done anything other than hang around with the wrong people. No reason it should ruin my life.

It was almost like coming home when they accepted me at the Centre. Maxine's is on Abercrombie Street, between Redfern station and the Centre, so I'd grab a coffee on the way to work. Sunlight bathed the front of the cafe in the mornings, and the entire front could be opened, with the windows accordioning together against one wall. There was a yellow and orange striped awning to give a bit of shade, and the outdoor seating was deckchairs beside little chopped up building palettes for tables.

Inside were a few stools against one wall and one tiny table with a chair reserved for staff. And, like I said, the best coffee in Sydney. Period. When I started work at the Centre, I went every morning, and sometimes in the afternoon too. The place was so chill; it was like a little holiday every day.

I felt old, but in a good way, when I went there. Like an older brother, maybe. All the students with their bags and laptops and eager chatter. I was only a few years older than them, but those years made all the difference: I was a working man. They were still kids.

Some of the chicks were hot, too. Whew! I'd grab a coffee on the way to work in the mornings, my hair still wet from the shower, and feel almost tender watching them pass by, ready to take on the world. Good luck, kids, eh? All baggy t-shirts and shiny over-ear headphones. They were so cute.

More Asians than I remembered from when I was a student. I suppose that's the way the world is going, but when you've been out in the world, getting crushed by all the crap of dealing with people, it's nice to see kids convinced the world is their oyster, even if they are from abroad.

At the beginning, I wondered what I'd do if I bumped into anyone from my uni days, but it never happened. So most days I'd grab lunch at Maxine's, too. A toasted focaccia, or an organic pumpkin soup with sourdough bread, or something, while the girls chatted amongst themselves or peeled off bandages to flaunt their new tattoos. It was all chill.

And then things kicked off at work.

I'd been thinking something was going to happen. You know what it's like. Everyone's on their best behaviour for six months and then the masks come off. So what, if technically I wasn't qualified? I had three years of a four-year degree, and you're expected to exaggerate on your CV. They could see I was able to do the job. It's not like there were more complaints about me than about anyone else.

But it was always me who got it in the neck.

Luckily, Paul, who ran Maxine's, was a mate. He was a miserable git, but I let him ramble on whenever he felt like it. Mind you, I knew more about coffee than he did, even though I limited myself to two cups a day. Sometimes only one, if I wasn't feeling good. It got me hyper. That's what it was for, of course.

So I kept coming around to Maxine's, even though the coffee was on the pricey side. Let Paul talk, and kept my head down, until he said he'd give me a chance. I got a couple of shifts and they went well.

Obviously.

I mean, I could do the job in my sleep. Make coffee and chat with customers. That's my thing. I'm great with people.

It was disappointing, of course. It was a step down from an office job, and just as I had thought I was leaving the past behind me, but whatever. I mean, working at Maxine's was almost like being on holiday and getting paid for it, too. How cool was that? Paul kept telling me to leave the chicks alone, but he was just jealous, I reckon. It's not like I did anything. Just being friendly. But I should have known Paul was going to be a dick to work for. Always watching me, so I made sure to do everything the exact way he told me, and stayed away from the till and the tip jar, if I wasn't dropping money in.

That's something they all watch for. Take it from me.

I preferred shifts with Dave because Dave stayed in the kitchen to do the food, leaving me to handle the coffee and the chat. The customers loved me.

Unlike Paul, who was always on my back. Six months, then the honeymoon's over, right? I think the lowest point was when I asked him if we could start using the cold brew dripper again and he said no. I was dying to get my hands on it. All the coffee I was drinking was doing my stomach in. Cold pressed would've gone down well. Less acid, you know? But he said it wasn't worth the hassle.

"You're the boss," I said.

That's when this little guy came in. He went and sat at the reserved table. A small man wearing a flat red woollen cap, like a knitted beret, and a red shirt. The clothes looked dirty, but when I went over, I just smelled detergent. So, an old hippie then, thank Christ. A bloody homeless was all I needed right then.

He had his legs crossed and his hands folded together in his lap. Any other day, I'd tell him the table was reserved, but screw Paul for being a dick. Let him say something. Which he didn't. It was always me he picked on, nobody else. The little guy looked familiar. Not like a friend of mine, but a friend of someone I knew, if that makes sense? I could imagine him outside the garage drinking tinnies with my dad. That kind of familiar.

And I liked him. He brought a bit of real life in among all these stuck-up students and yuppies and the rest of them.

I brought him a coffee on the house when Paul went into the kitchen. I was wondering if it was worth all the aggravation. You don't get rich on tips when most of your customers are students. And then Paul went and surprised me, asked if I could handle a shift on my own the next day. I felt like hugging him for trusting me. That's why he had been going so hard on me; he wanted to make sure I could handle the pressure.

I said yes. I nearly wept, I swear.

He was going to be best man for a surfer mate, who was getting married, and had to head off to Angourie Point for the stag do. He'd asked Chris first, but Chris and Dave had both come down with something, so I'd be on my own. I told him not to worry, I could handle it. For a moment he even looked happy, the miserable git. Excited to get out of town and leave his missus behind, I reckon.

Dirty bugger. Good luck to him.

I couldn't wait. With no one around to cramp my style, I'd be able to shine.

I got up extra early and had a coffee at home. Opened up Maxine's and had another one before I pulled the shutter back. Hoping I wouldn't regret it, I treated myself to a third coffee while serving the first customers.

It was awesome.

I used to be one of these poor sods, running from the crowded train to the dead air of the office, stressing over every second of delay at the cafe. Now, look at me. I bloody *was* the cafe. Sun shining. Pretty girls. Office guys in gelled hair giving me respect, because they needed my caffeine fix.

Here you go, bro. I just saved your life.

Christ! Imagine having to sit through meeting after meeting with Chad after Chad, without a good cup of coffee inside you. I was a bloody saint.

I was also shaking from the caffeine, but that didn't stop me from having another one to celebrate dealing with the morning rush. After that, I needed a sit down before lunch started and, well, what else am I going to do? I had a coffee.

Sharone from next door came in while I was sitting at the staff table and after she paid, we got into a minor discussion of how much change she thought I owed her. I didn't make a big deal out of it. The customer is always right, and all that. I'd just overcharge her for something else.

Face like a slapped arse when she left, though.

She had ruined the mood, and I didn't even notice my little homeless buddy in the red cap come in. I made him a Macchiato on the house, because there was no one around to stop me.

Greg from the barbershop over the road came in for tea and a muffin. He's been coming here for years. I hate him.

Best coffee in Sydney, and he always orders tea.

Friday is normally good, because the mornings are packed, but the afternoon is quiet when the students go home. But I was struggling by then, and my insides were burning with the bitter aftertaste of old coffee from my stomach all the way up to the back of my throat. I knew Sharone would make a big deal about me messing up the change, and Greg was *looking* at me over his bloody tea cup.

I don't think it was busier than usual, but I was sweating like a pig, and cursing Dave for getting sick: I could have used his help. Paul had arranged for some extra food, and a sign which said "Sorry! Limited Service!" but that didn't stop people from asking me for soup and other crap.

The only person not getting on my tits was my buddy in the beret.

He sat at the staff table as good as gold, sipping his coffee and watching life go by. The perfect customer.

Meanwhile, I was in tatters behind the counter because I needed to piss, and the sun was shining in, and today was the one day of the year that everybody decided to pay in small coins. They kept flashing the sun into my eyes, blinding me. I kept having to ask, "What did you give me again?" like an idiot. I just wanted to do a good job, but it was such a dick move for Paul to take a Friday off.

Practically our busiest day.

Things calmed down after lunch, but the place was a mess. I tried clearing a table and dropped the cups, jittery from the coffee. So I retreated behind the counter, where I felt safer.

I was feeling better as the clock ticked towards three o'clock, while I chatted with this history student. I don't know history, but she was cute, and the place was practically empty. This is what I was good at, turning random customers into regulars.

I made us both a coffee and sat with her. It was just the two of us, some random guy with massive headphones squashing a huge blonde quiff on his head, and my little mate in the red beret at the back. Me and the girl were having a laugh, and some people can't stand to see that. Other people enjoying themselves.

Next thing I know, Squashed Quiff was behind me, up real close, with his hands out, like he knows karate, telling me to back off, leave her alone. I mean, what? We were just talking. When I looked at the chick, I could see she was upset. Well, of course she was. The guy must have been a psycho.

She was in tears and Mr Quiff was shouting at me, asking me what my problem was. If someone had come in at that moment, it would have looked like *I* had done something to upset her. She ran off while I was dealing with him.

Wanted to get away before the creep could follow her home, I reckon.

Well, I gave her a couple of minutes' head start before I kicked him out—not too gently, either—and then just closed up. It was as good as closing time, anyway. My hands were still shaking as I chained the outside chairs and tables together.

It'll give you some idea of the state I was in, when I tell you I'd forgotten about the little guy at the back, until I came in and saw him sitting in the gloom of the shuttered cafe. He seemed happy enough, though, so I left him alone while I started clearing the tables. I didn't want to deal with any more people. I was fuming with Paul for taking a break before I was ready.

Sure, I'd agreed, but what else was I going to say?

You ready to mind the shop?

No.

No worries, mate. Don't let the door hit you on the way out!

I mean, I could do it, normally, but not when people are just being awful like today. I was too bloody sensitive, I suppose. I was angry with all of them, even the history chick. She had long brown hair, which I like, and a short upper lip, which showed her teeth. Made her look into what I was saying. So cute! But Sharone would complain about me when Paul got back, and I was sure DJ Quiff would be back to tell Paul his fictional version of events, as revenge for me kicking him out. I was going to have some explaining to do. No problem, I'd tell him what really happened, but I hate that it's always me who attracts the nutters, you know?

I was going to have to chase the little guy out too, now, and I just knew that he'd kick off as well. That's the kind of day it was, right? I went to the bathroom first and splashed water on my face. Took some deep breaths. Came back out and made myself a coffee.

"Where's Maxine?" he asked me when I went up to him.

I stared at him. *What the…?* "Maxine's not here, mate," I said. "Come back tomorrow."

"Tomorrow?" He said it like there wouldn't be one. Joker.

"What do you need Maxine for?"

"Me? I'm asking you, mate. Where's Maxine?"

I was so sick of it. "There's no Maxine. It's my cafe, I just made the name up. And now we're closed and—" You know what? It had never even occurred to me to wonder who Maxine was until he'd asked.

"I'm going for a drink," he said. "You coming?"

"Thanks, mate." *Was he serious?* "But I've got to finish tidying my cafe."

He held my eye. I knew him. Definitely.

I think.

"You're shaking," he said.

I was. I'd just gone behind the counter to switch off the machine and couldn't believe the state of the place. Paul would have had a fit. It looked like I'd been trying to build a sand pit out of damp coffee grounds. The cloth for wiping off the milk steamer was draped over the muffins. If Paul had seen that, it would have given him a heart attack after he'd recovered from his fit. I tried to remember when I'd draped it there. It must have been early on, because we always sold out of muffins. Did I sell one to Greg? I couldn't remember too much about the day, as a matter of fact. Coffee does that to me. There was another dishcloth hanging in the milk jug, two on the floor, and milk everywhere. I glanced into the kitchen at the piles of plates in the sink and whatever *that* was in the corner. I needed to get cleaning, but I was so wound up I'd probably make matters worse.

And hell, I was the boss today. I could nip across, have one to calm down, and then tidy up. Get the place spotless before Dave showed up in the morning.

Of course, if he'd been here, the place wouldn't even be in a mess. I had half a mind to leave it for him.

Not that I'd do that, of course. I was just in a funny mood.

We went to the Glengarry, as it was closest. He sat me down and—get this—he bought me a beer! How cool of him was that? Then he buggered off to feed coins to the pokies near the back of the hotel. I stayed where I was and sipped beer. I'd finish and then head back.

"Good boy," he said, when he returned. I think he was talking to me, but he had a big paper cup full of coins, so he could have been referring to the slot machines. "Hold out your hands."

I did so, and he tipped coins into them.

"Get the drinks in."

I stood up, concentrating on not dropping any. I hadn't eaten since breakfast and I needed to go, but you have to get your round in.

"Where's Maxine?" He didn't look at me as he asked, just whispered it as I stood to get the drinks.

I didn't know, and I didn't much care.

The first beer calmed my stomach, and the second helped me relax, but it was niggling at me. I'd have to get back to the cafe, but I wanted to know what his story was with Maxine. Maybe he was an old boyfriend or something.

He was a good laugh, so I stayed a bit longer. He chatted with everyone, though he only ever asked me who Maxine was. At some point, the bouncer kicked us out. Didn't I say it was one of those days?

We hadn't done anything, so I reckon my mate had won too much on the pokies. No worries, we went to the off-licence. We could drink outside just as well as inside, and we still had a load of change from his winnings.

He was a proper gentleman, despite the stupid beret.

"Where's Maxine?" he asked, as we sat in the park.

I wouldn't get back to the cafe tonight. I'd go first thing in the morning before anyone arrived.

It might sound weird (or it may have been the drink), but the more he asked about Maxine, the less it annoyed me. I *did* know who he was talking about. It was like he was trying to help, like some kind of shock therapist. I wondered who had arranged for him to come see me. Only vaguely, because I was trying to count the number of tins we had left and divide the answer by two. We couldn't open the voddy until we had finished them, he'd said.

"I've never seen her at the cafe," I said. I was trying to work out who she was via elimination.

"That's obvious, mate." He waved a hand to encompass me sitting in the park in the dark, on my arse, with an old boozer. He chuckled.

I didn't get it. Maybe I knew her from uni, or the Centre? But I didn't like to think about that. Those were bad days. Forget them and move on.

Where's Maxine? Where's Maxine?

I pulled two beers out of the paper bag and popped them open. Offered the guy one. We drank.

You could always find someone to talk to around Redfern. It wasn't the most reputable neighbourhood, but nothing like it used to be, back in the day. Plenty of police around, too, but just showing their faces to keep the professionals moving in from Newtown happy. Mostly they keep driving. Me and the little guy were talking to this girl—well, woman—but she dressed younger, you know? We were walking her home, chatting, but the cops slowed, watching us, and that made her nervous and she sped up. Almost made it look like we were chasing her, so we left it. I don't force my company on anyone. Just trying to do the right thing. There are some right nutters around at night.

And it was proper night by now. Everything was shut but then we met this other girl—well, woman—in the park and she was good fun, and it was too far in for the police to come, so we were having a laugh, and I was pleased with my little mate.

He'd turned the day right around for me.

I was starting to feel like he was my best buddy in all the world, when the chick asked me back to her place, just around the corner.

Hopefully, he'd do the right thing and piss off. Really, I just wanted to sleep for a couple of hours before heading in to clean the cafe, but if she wanted, we could mess around a bit first. She looked all right for an old lady.

She shouldn't laugh so much with all those missing teeth, but otherwise, yeah, not bad.

I couldn't shake him off, though. Fair enough, he had paid for the booze, so it was his party, too. I tried giving him a signal, but he didn't notice.

She lived past the station and around the corner. And then around another corner, and then maybe another one, or else she got lost. But we found it eventually. There was a gutted armchair out front, under a jacaranda tree. Its dropped purple flowers rustled under our feet as we hung around, waiting for her to open the door.

It gave me goosebumps.

The door led straight in off the street. "You go in first," my mate says.

I didn't like the way he looked at me.

I know some guys get off on having their mates around, but that wasn't me. And I could see he was expecting something. Something bad. But he was behind me, and the chick was in front, and I didn't want to scare her by making a fuss, so I went in.

I sobered a bit up at the thought that something was wrong and felt sorry for the old girl who was doing us a favour by letting us crash at her place. She pointed us to the front room, which she said was where her kid crashed whenever he came around to visit. My mate went in and lay down.

"I'll see you boys in the morning," she said, and creaked upstairs.

That was it.

I lay on the couch in the living room, able to breathe again, inhaling the smell of cigarettes and fried food. It took me back. Especially with the old girl upstairs and my old mate in the next room. I tried to stay awake for a while, in case she was just being discreet, waiting for him to nod off, but then I dozed off.

It was still dark when my mate woke me. "Where's Maxine?" he asked. I pretended I was still asleep, and he padded out of the room again.

"Where's Maxine?" The sky was getting bright outside the window when he woke me the second time.

"Christ, mate!" I had a headache. He was leaning over me, looking down. So I stood up. There was only a messy backyard visible through the living room window, so I went into the kid's bedroom at the front of the house to see if I could work out where we'd ended up. Just some narrow street, barely wide enough for two cars to pass each other. The jaded Victorian houses leaned into each other from either side, making the street gloomy. Too early for even the first joggers to be about.

The old girl was still asleep upstairs. And my mate was sneaking up towards her.

Oh Christ, I thought, *this is what it had all been about.* He was some mad serial rapist. Maybe he was even going to kill her.

Then blame it all on me.

I stayed where I was. I could run for it as soon as he was out of sight.

Then he turned to beckon me to come with him.

I shook my head.

"Come on," he said.

I shook my head.

He called me again, and again, louder each time. "Come on, Ian! Come on! Come on, Ian!"

And I didn't know his name, but he knew mine, so I was going to be forced to watch him kill a little old lady. I didn't want to, but I didn't want him to wake her and scare her, either. Especially as now she'd know my name, too.

Maybe he could kill her in her sleep. That would be best, wouldn't it?

That way, she wouldn't even notice anything. So I went up the stairs after him, to keep him quiet. That way, she wouldn't suffer. Because I'm not a bad person, I just hang around with the wrong people, which always gets me in trouble.

We were standing on the landing at the top of the stairs by now, and I was holding my breath. I told myself to let it go. To take a deep breath, but I couldn't. My throat wasn't working, and the lack of oxygen made my heart pound in my temples. I didn't want to kill an old woman who had done nothing to me. She was still snoring, thank God. We could leave before anything bad happened.

"Come on, mate!" I said. "I have to get to the cafe."

But my mate, the mad rapist, was still looking for his woman, wasn't he? "Where's Maxine?" he asked me.

I had a brainwave. "Maxine's at the cafe, mate. Come on, let's go see her," I said.

It was worth a try.

He pushed at the bedroom door. It swung open, releasing the smell of cheap perfume, talcum powder and old jumpers onto the landing. He looked at me like I was the biggest idiot he'd ever met, and I was, wasn't I?

How did I get from a couple of coffees to here? The door was slowing, with the old woman safely on one side, and a lunatic on the other. We stood close together in the warm, cramped hallway landing and it felt like an experiment. You know the one. With the cat in the box with the poison?

If the door stopped less than halfway open, we'd all get out of here. But if it swung past that, there would be bloodshed. It stopped exactly halfway.

"Come on, mate. The cafe," I whispered, and headed towards the stairs. He followed me, and I'd just saved the old girl's life! I was a bloody hero, and nobody'd ever know. It was always me who got in trouble, but nobody cared when I did the right thing.

He was quiet, but followed me all the way.

I needed a coffee.

And what wouldn't I give for a cop car to pull us over? *Alright, guys? What are you blokes doing at this time of the morning?* No sign of them. Everything left to me to sort out. All I wanted was to go home and sleep, but no chance with this psycho behind me.

Mind you, nothing had actually happened, had it?

Maybe he had just been going to ask her where his Maxine was. Maybe I was letting the stress get to me. But there was no doubt that things had got away from me, and I was pissed at Paul for letting it happen, and with Dave for wimping out.

———

When we made it back to the cafe, I realised I'd forgotten to lock the bloody door. In a flash, I was stone cold sober. In the instant where the door swung open, all the booze drained out of my system.

But then, although the place was a mess, nothing was missing. It hadn't been robbed or trashed. Everything was fine.

I whooped in relief. Big mistake.

Sharone already had her newsagent's open, and she came over to see what the fuss was. She saw me, and she saw the state of the cafe, and I knew it was all over.

I'd been working so hard to keep everything running, but she'd tell Paul and that was it. Some people never catch a break. It was always me who grabbed the dirty end of the stick.

"Where's Maxine?" asked my little buddy. He'd gone in while I was still in the doorway, trying to block Sharone from seeing any more. I'd forgotten about him again. "*He'd* know what to do."

He? "Maxine is a...?" I stopped. Because in my head it was like when that picture of a white candleholder suddenly flips into two black faces staring at each other. I *knew.*

"Well done, Ian," he said. His voice was quiet. The patient teacher who had finally got the class dummy to understand the lesson. "We need him."

Sharone was on one side of me, saying something I couldn't hear, and my little mate was on the other, surrounded by the debris of yesterday's disaster. I'd had enough, hadn't I?

You saw me. I took care of *everything.* All by myself. And just because things got a bit out of hand, I was going to get the blame and the boot.

Just like at uni, just like at the Centre, same as always.

I'd saved a woman's life this morning, but Sharone didn't care. She'd never liked me. Paul had never liked me either. He was just using me to skip off at the first opportunity. I wasn't cut out for this dog-eat-dog world. Only my mate in the stupid beret had stuck with me, and he wanted to talk to Max.

"Where's Max, Ian?"

And Max was right there.

He was a nasty piece of work, but he never let a mate down. He was there for me after uni, and he was there for me after the Centre, and he was here now.

I was going to cop it, anyway. Paul had probably decided to fire me as soon as he'd driven off. *I'll let the poor sucker bust his guts while I have fun, and fire him first thing when I get back!* I could hear him.

Yeah, well, he hadn't reckoned on Max being here to help me out. Max wasn't sensitive like I was. Max was the part of me that did what it wanted. The part that ruined everything, but that I couldn't live without. I got pissed on, Max pissed petrol back, then threw his ciggie into the puddle as he walked away. And if I was annoyed at Paul, Max was furious.

The little guy helped us pull all the cafe's furniture into a pile, helped us smash all the glass. He even had a little can of lighter fuel ready in his pocket. A little can, because he was a little guy, ha, ha! But that's all you need, if you know what you're doing.

And it was he who got rid of Sharone, when she started banging on the door again because of all the noise.

I made us a last cup of coffee before we left. It had been a long night. Best coffee in Sydney. Used to be, anyway. After I made it, I opened the cash register out of habit. Yeah, you've already guessed. That's where my little mate had really gotten the money for the drinks, but it didn't matter at this stage.

We lit the lighter fuel and strolled outside. The sun was shining. It was early, so there was a chill in the air, but with the heat and the glow of the flames chewing through the building, it was warm. Almost like being on holidays.

It was creepy at first. He just kept staring at us. At me, because everyone else was ignoring him. But Jen said he wasn't doing anything, just leave it. Jen gave money to, like, all the homeless. She joked about doing it to motivate me to finish Uni and get a good job, so I could afford to keep her in the style to which she had become accustomed. Otherwise, she would have to marry Ross.

I didn't think it was funny. She used to go out with Ross, so it was in poor taste, if you ask me. But Uni didn't start for another couple of weeks, and I wanted to relax, so I ignored the homeless guy as best I could. We were on the beach, just drinking some beers and messing about. Having fun.

After a while he came over, and that was good, because even Jen got uptight when the homeless come too close. He smelled all right though, so maybe he was some old hippie or something. He looked like it, with his faded shirt and beret cap. I almost expected a French accent when he spoke. Some artist who had come over years ago and got too stoned to leave. There were loads of French around Maroubra. But he didn't say much, and he didn't have an accent. Probably just wanted some company, poor sod. I decided to forget him. No point getting worked up.

He was still hanging around when we left. Not his fault, but the mood had gone sour. Jen was flirting with Ross, even though she knew I hated that. I wasn't the jealous type, but that's the problem, isn't it?

If I say something then it looks like I can't take a joke, because they're old friends, right? And if I say nothing, it looks like I don't care that my girlfriend is acting like a slut. I mean, Jesus! It's always my fault.

The others headed off to their cars, and Jen walked to the cafe with me. I was doing the late shift, and it was all good. I'd text her later, and we'd be sorted before I even got home. But then the look she gave me told me that a couple of emojis wouldn't cut it. *Come on!* It was, like, I was the one putting all the effort in, and yet it was still me who had to keep apologising. Unbelievable.

"We'll talk later, Lee," she said, and went home.

I was thinking, *Ah, screw it!* I might not even go home. Finish my shift, hit the clubs, plenty more fish in the sea and all that, yeah?

I didn't even notice the little Frenchie had followed me until he asked me a question.

He said: "Where's Ashley?"

Visitation

I like this story, with its neat merging of the otherworldly and the mundane.
I must have dreamed it, because it popped out of my pen almost fully formed first thing when I woke up one morning (Tuesday, the 10th of August, 2021, for those interested).
So, the question is: how long do I need to sleep to get a full 80,000 word novel?

The knifeman sharpened knives, polished tableware, and, from the reflections in their surfaces, told fortunes.

In the precise flash of a knife's blade, he knew how long someone had left to live. In the round contour of a plate or pot, he could spot fat dowries, or husbands.

The lady of the house received him as an honoured guest in poor households, the butler or housekeeper in rich ones, where he could expect to do his work seated in the butler's own chair.

When he left, people gossiped quietly together, sharing their futures—if he had given them one—away from the ears of the priest, who despised the scarecrow figure and greased curls of the knifeman.

Joan was Father Brier's kitchen maid. She was new to the role. New enough to claim ignorance if the priest complained she had let the knifeman into his house. Her older sister, Mary, had been the priest's kitchen maid until she passed away the week before.

"You want to know what happened to your sister?" asked the knifeman.

Joan shook her head.

"You want to know if she's happy where she is now?"

Joan would have liked to hear that her sister was happy and looking down fondly, but the knifeman only allowed one vision.

"You want to know what will happen to you?"

"To *him,*" she said.

The priest's household was small, as befit a humble man of God. As she had no butler's place to offer him in the rectory, Joan led the knifeman to the church's altar to perform his work. He had finished polishing the paten for the Eucharist and started on the chalice before the priest discovered him.

The knifeman's soft green leather cloth hissed over the chalice. He ignored the priest behind him, whose reflection on the surface of the chalice swelled obscenely as he approached. Instead, the knifeman stared into it to see what would happen.

The priest felt physically repulsed to see the knifeman handling the sacred instrument, though the sound of the polishing was hypnotic, soothing. He stepped closer, wondering why he never polished the chalice like this himself. His reflection morphed, his belly swelling, his head shrinking to a dot near the lip of the chalice as he came to stand behind the knifeman. The cloth continued to hiss over the metal and the priest, who also worked with visions and the afterlife, saw the chalice fill with blood.

The body of Mary, Joan's sister, floated naked, face down in it.

That's how he knew the knifeman was a devil. No one other than himself and God had known about his relationship with Mary. He'd sworn her to silence for the good of the town. He'd have married her gladly if he hadn't found her too late, made his vows to God many years before. Otherwise they could have been happy together, watched their child grow up safe and loved.

But his God, though loving, was strict. He had destroyed the unbelieving Israelites, the cities of Sodom and Gomorrah, banished his own angels to everlasting darkness when they sinned. This town, with its gossip and veniality, could not expect to escape God's vengeance, having once drawn his ire. His own happiness was the price the priest paid to keep them all safe.

He had drowned Mary in the font, after filling it with holy water, to wash away her sin. After blessing her, he held her head underwater until she stopped struggling. She was happy now, and everyone was safe.

Only a devil would remind him of how much he longed to join with her again. The priest backed away, hoping to escape the monster who dared defile the chalice.

The knifeman kept his back to the priest, watching his form distort and roil in the reflective surface.

In the gold, he saw Joan enter the church behind the priest. Saw the priest meet his fate on the point of the knife she held.

After he finished polishing the chalice, he put it away with the paten and left.

He had already sharpened the knives that morning.

Granny's Well

If you go down to the woods today, prepare for a giallo-tinged retelling of the Red Riding Hood story.
Don't believe the fake news.
This is what really went down when the wolf showed up at Granny's house.

———

"This is real good of you, Red," said Wolf.

"Oh, my pleasure," she said, her voice even huskier than usual.

They'd been caught out by the sudden late summer storm. Wolf had arrived first at the Granny's cottage. No one had answered the bell, so he had stayed on the doormat inside the front hall, hopping from one foot to another and shivering, but shy about going in further. Then Red had showed up, sopping wet and breathless. She'd dug out some towels and handed him one, before towelling her hair dry as best she could without taking off the hood she always wore.

The cottage was cosy, with a fire blazing in the hearth. Which was a bad idea in an unattended cottage in the middle of a forest, but perhaps Granny had figured a storm was nature's own fire brigade. Rain and branches crowded around the cottage, tapping insistently on the window to be let in, and the table was set for two. Wolf guessed Red normally came around this time to visit her Granny, who'd probably popped off to the shop to get some bottled water.

Wolf remembered Red joking about her Granny going yuppie and only drinking water from bottles these days, even though she had a working well in her front garden. Plenty of water in it too. Wolf had passed it on his way to the front door, and it was overflowing because of the storm. He wouldn't normally barge in at all, but the wind and rain had been fierce, and he was terrified of thunder. He checked his paws. They were wet but not muddy, though he'd gone right past the well. He'd have hated to have tracked mud into Granny's house.

"I should boil some water or something for tea," said Wolf. "Granny'll be soaking when she comes back." He always felt nervous around Red. He still had the same crush on her as when he was a cub. Most of the wolves in the forest did. Not that there were many of them left, anymore. The forest was a dangerous place these days. Maybe it was something in the air, making everyone act differently. Wolf was sure he could hear a woodpecker or something still tapping away close by, despite the terrible weather.

"Don't worry, Granny's fine," said Red. "But I'm glad we bumped into each other. How come I don't see you around so much anymore?"

"Just busy, Red."

In fact, with the forest being such a small place, he'd gone to considerable trouble to stay out of her way. The forest was going through dark days, especially now the Purists were running the council. The carefree days when a wolf and a girl could be friends were long gone.

"I've missed you, Wolf," said Red. "It's almost like you've been avoiding me."

Wolf swallowed, wondering if he'd heard her right. She looked different: thinner and sadder. Older. She smelled different, and her voice was strained. He added some logs to the fire, in case she was catching a cold. She still had those big brown eyes that ran in her family though, the ones that made the butterflies in his stomach lift off and do synchronised fluttering.

She meant she missed him as a friend, of course. It was too dangerous for them to be anything more than that. In the warm cottage, with the heat of the flames licking his fur, it was a pleasant daydream to think she could have meant it otherwise, though.

"Come here," said Red, "you're dripping on the floor." She patted the space on the rose-patterned couch beside her, then held out her towel to him.

The stink of his own wet fur dampened all other smells, but his heart skipped a beat at the thought of drying himself with a towel that held her scent. He took the towel but sat down in an armchair instead.

A flash of lightning lit up her face, and he saw she was wearing thick makeup, which might explain why she didn't smell the same. After the flash, the cottage was dim and intimate again.

In the soft firelight, her red hood, which she never, ever took off, glowed a deep blood red, with strands of auburn hair curling out underneath it. The rain, or whatever it was, continued tapping.

"I brought wine and cheese for Granny, but there's more than enough for all of us."

"That might not be a good idea," said Wolf, dizzy at her proximity, at the way the evening seemed to be shaping up. "I should go look for Granny. Do you hear that tapping?" It was starting to get on his nerves. To his overwrought ears it sounded urgent, almost like a warning. "I could see if there's a leak somewhere."

"What's up?" said Red. "You don't like me anymore? We used to be very close." She poured wine from the open bottle on the table and handed him a glass.

Wolf took it and wondered what was happening. What would Granny think if she came back now? What if someone else came in? A girl and a wolf having what looked like a romantic meal, that'd get them both in big trouble.

Something wasn't right here.

"What happened, Wolf? I thought you had a huge crush on me. You're not one of these Purist species bigots, are you?"

"Look, I'm not the bad guy here," said Wolf. He sniffed at his glass. The wine had notes of grape and… something else. He wasn't an expert on fruit. It tickled his nose, but in a good way.

"Oh, no?" said the Woodsman, who was suddenly standing behind them. There are few places louder than a forest in the middle of a storm and neither of them had heard him come in. "What's up, little girl?" The Woodsman wore glasses, thick as the bottoms of Coke bottles. They were spattered in rain, which slid down the lenses to collect at the bottom.

"Little girl? Jee-zus!" said Wolf.

"Problem?"

"We were actually talking here," said Wolf.

"Yeah, well, it's pissing fifteen shades of hell outside so… are you crying, Red?"

"I don't want to talk about it, Woodie."

"What did you do, Wolf?"

"I came in out of the storm, same as you."

"Sure you did. You saw little Red all by herself and thought you'd get yourself some of that. Animal. Always after what you can't have. You stick with your own kind, Wolf, and there'll be no trouble."

"Red and I are friends," said Wolf.

"Red's too nice, is what it is. You wolves been having your way too long around here, then disappearing off to the city when things get hard."

"Yeah? There aren't too many woodsmen left in the forest either, is what I hear."

The Woodsman faced Wolf, but with the firelight glinting off his glasses, there was no way to tell if he was really staring at him, or just thinking and staring into space. Wolf stared back anyway, his eyes sore in the dry heat from the fire, until the Woodsman came over and sat on the arm of the couch beside Red. He sat so close that Red had to shuffle sideways to prevent him from sitting on her.

He was a big man, his upper arms were as thick as Wolf's chest. Wolf had made an effort to stay out of Red's way, but an even bigger one to stay out of Woodie's way. The Woodsman was a psycho, as well as being half-blind, which made him a dangerous person to bump into, especially since he'd taken up with the Purist idiots, who believed in a hierarchy of species. Every species should know their place. And obviously humans—Purists—sat at the top of the pile.

Wolf had been woken a few months back by the wet thump of an axe against a tree. He had seen no one, but the word "Mongrel" had been blazed into the bole of a tree close to his house. It could have been anyone, but he'd bumped into Woodie the day before. That was around the time he started avoiding Red. No sense in getting her in trouble, too. He could keep his head down and, if things got worse, he could always move to the city, while Red was stuck here for as long as she needed to keep checking Granny was alright.

"Don't be scared, Red. I'm here now." The Woodsman picked up Wolf's glass, sniffed at it, then tossed all the wine back in one go. He rested his huge hand with its thick fingers like juicy pork and apple sausages on Red's shoulder.

"Hey, I only came here to get out of the weather," said Wolf. "Did you guys see the well overflowing? It's really coming down." He stood. "Let's go look for Granny. She could be in trouble."

"Wolf shows up and Granny's in trouble. That sounds about right," said the Woodsman.

"Are you serious? Read the papers. It's wolves and woodsmen in trouble these days. The forest doesn't like either of us anymore, Woodie."

"That's what happens when animals want more than they deserve." His axe still rested on his shoulder. Now he stretched his spine and rolled the handle between his fingers, so that the blade twirled, throwing out a disco ball of glinting light. With his other hand, he started kneading Red's shoulder, all the while staring at Wolf through his thick glasses.

There was something really wrong here, and the ongoing tapping wasn't helping with Wolf's paranoia.

Red's lips twitched, but he couldn't tell if it was because Woodie was squeezing too tightly or just right.

Wasn't she worried about Granny?

Wolf's skin crawled, making his fur bush up. This wasn't the Red he knew. And he knew her well. He'd even kissed her once, years ago, during a game of Spin the Bottle. Her teeth had been small and her excited breath had been hot and sweet.

But he'd never told her how he'd felt. Maybe that's where he'd gone wrong. All the wolves—the woodsmen, too—had been in love with Red, but only he'd been lucky enough to kiss her.

Or unlucky, perhaps, because he'd never been able to get over her after that.

Perhaps she was nervous now, caught alone with him by old-fashioned Woodie. Who knew? It might be she even believed some of that Purist crap, now. He needed to keep his eye on Woodie, though, who was breathing heavily, looking for an excuse to swing his dumb axe.

"Granny's fine, Wolf," said Red. "I was dropping off some wine and cheese for her. She'll be back when this is all over." Thunder boomed overhead. Red turned to the Woodsman. "Wolf was already here when I arrived. We were talking about old times, before he started getting personal."

"Me? You were the one who brought up the past, talking about how I used to have a huge—"

"Woodie!" said Red. "He's lying! Thank God you came in. He was trying to get me drunk!"

"Okay…" said Wolf. "Let's go over what we know. There's a storm outside, yes? So I came in and then you guys came in and actually there is something strange going on, because—"

He pushed hard off the ground, tipping his armchair over backwards. He rolled over its back and sprang onto his feet, ready to jump again. He had only just avoided Woodie's axe, which now swung towards him a second time.

Red was backing towards the front door. She didn't look scared, although her face was lined with tension, her lips hanging open. She backed away until she was standing against the front door. If Wolf made a break for it, Woodie would think he was going after her.

Wolf dived backwards to avoid the Woodsman's next swing.

Red yelled and locked the front door. Maybe it was the uncertain light of the thunder and the fire, but Red looked ill. She suddenly looked a lot older than the Red he'd been in love with for so long.

"*You* got here first? Well, now, Mr Wolf—" The Woodsman was flexing his neck and stalking towards him, herding him towards the closed bedroom door.

Wolf hoped it wasn't locked. He rattled it with a paw. It was.

"It's just 'Wolf,' actually."

"—what a big heap of trouble you're in!" He swung his axe, two-handed, overhead.

Wolf sidestepped, and the blade crashed through the door to Granny's bedroom. Dust filled the air and tickled Wolf's nose.

Woodie grunted as he fought to free the blade, bits of wood tapping as they rained onto the floor.

With nowhere else to go, Wolf used the precious few seconds this gave him to punch out enough of the splinters to squeeze his way through the shattered door into the bedroom. There'd be a window in there, though he didn't relish diving through it.

"No!" said Red. "Not in there!"

"Don't worry, Red, this cur has eaten his last Granny!" With a shout, Woodie ploughed his axe through the remains of the door, then shoulder-charged through the frame.

This wasn't the way Wolf had ever imagined going. Getting taken out by a younger wolf, sure. A drunken knife-fight with a deer, perhaps. Maybe even mugged and sliced up by a pack of desperate badgers; the forest was getting more dangerous every year. But he'd never thought he'd be offed by a psycho while the girl he dreamed about watched like she couldn't wait. Boy, had he been wrong about her!

"Come on, you guys have known me for years. True, you've never *liked* me, Woodie, but really?"

"I don't know you," said Red, following them into the bedroom.

Wolf had tried the window, which had child locks on and no sign of the key. Now he was on the far side of the bed, where Red's picnic basket was. The bed was unmade, other than for a rubber sheet to protect the mattress.

So Granny had a weak bladder. So what?

But the tang of disinfectant and other smells in the room stung his nose. Even as Woodie came closer, trying a few low practice swings—and he was big enough for the axe to reach all the way over the large bed—pieces slotted together in Wolf's head.

Red's basket *beside the bed!*

Red was still watching the blade. Wolf needed to buy himself another few seconds to confirm what he was thinking.

"Seems to me you know all the wolves and woodsmen around here, Red," he said. "Or used to, before they disappeared. When was the last time you visited Granny?" Wolf was getting tired, trying to keep an eye on the strangely distant Red, while avoiding Woodie's axe.

"A few weeks ago." Red shrugged off the question.

"She seem all right?" Wolf's muscles ached, but his brain was spinning as it put everything together.

He checked the basket. No wine or cheese. It was piled with rocks, covered with a soft striped dishcloth.

The Woodsman feinted left, took a moment to catch his breath, then feinted right.

Wolf felt sick at the thoughts in his head. The tapping was even louder in here.

"Sure," said Red. "Since when is being eaten by a wolf a long-term illness?"

"There was a storm a couple of weeks ago." Wolf's mouth was dry.

"Sure. If you say so."

"Everybody shut up," said the Woodsman. Sweat was dripping down his forehead, and he had to keep pushing his glasses back up his slippery nose. "I'm going to wipe out this filthy mangy disease, then you and me are going to get married, Red. I don't care what your Granny says." He hefted the axe.

"Woodie, listen, you need to hear this!" Wolf held an urgent paw out, then paused. "Wait, what? Since when are you guys…?"

"Come on, Woodie," said Red. "Chop, chop!"

"Because that's about when the last wolf 'went to the city.' You remember, Woodie? You should do, because the woodcutter who lived beside you disappeared at the exact same time." Wolf ducked the low-flying roundhouse swipe only by flattening his snout into

Granny's bed. And recognised the stench that the disinfectant covered up.

"And a couple of weeks before that was another storm. The same week another wolf and another woodsman disappeared 'off to the city.'"

"If you're insinuating what I think you're insinuating, you sick pervert…" said Woodie.

"Oh Christ, Woodie! That's not it, keep up!" The two of them stared breathlessly at each other on either side of Granny's neatly stripped bed, with its rubber sheet. "I'll bet you came to visit Granny that night too, Red? With wine and cheese?"

The tapping had stopped as if the storm was listening.

"Could be," said Red.

"I say you did. And I'll bet you offered the wolf a glass of wine when you 'just showed up.'"

"Shut it, Wolf. Red's pure, she wouldn't drink with dogs!" But Woodie waited to find out where Wolf was going with this.

"But never mind, because luckily a woodsman came along in time to save you, right?"

"My noble brothers!" said the Woodsman, clapping his right hand to his heart.

"And then *he* got a glass of wine, right?"

"I'm bored, Wolf. I drank some wine, too. What's your point?"

"Well, why not ask Red where her basket is?"

"What?"

"She came round to check Granny was well. She brought wine and cheese, remember?"

"So?"

Wolf's eyes hunted around the room as the tapping started up again. *There!* The large cupboard. "So, when she turned up at the door tonight, she didn't have a basket."

"Then where'd the wine come from, Wolf?" said Woodie, as if Wolf had tripped himself up.

"Exactly!" Wolf pointed a triumphant finger at him, and Woodie took a half-hearted swing at it. "It was already there, on the table. Like she'd been expecting company. And her basket is *here*, even though the bedroom door has been closed this entire time."

"What are you trying to pull, Wolf?" He made a sudden jump, clearing the bed and almost catching Wolf, who darted around the bed towards Red, grabbing her before she could run, using her as a shield so he could keep talking to Woodie.

"You know what they do when an animal's endangered? They put it on the Red List."

"So?" The Woodsman's eyes normally looked huge behind his glasses, but now they were screwed up, as if he was concentrating, or trying to keep them open.

"So, you know how long it is since I met another wolf? I think both of us are already on the Red List. Or should I say, the Granny List!"

With a flourish, Wolf ripped Red's riding hood off. With it came a wig and false eyelashes, while globs of makeup wiped off onto his hairy forearm.

It wasn't Red who'd been sweet talking him tonight; it had been Granny. That was why she'd smelled wrong.

And not just Wrong Person wrong, but Crazy Person wrong. She struggled in Wolf's grasp, then sank her teeth into his arm.

"Red, no!" cried Woodie and swung his axe, forcing Wolf to dive backwards, cracking his head against the wall, in order to save both himself and Granny from the blow. "What has he done to you?"

"It's Granny, you fool!" Wolf scrabbled for the light switch. Perhaps it was too dark for Woodie to recognise her.

Woodie swung again, but he was slowing down, and looked ready to fall asleep on his feet. His head kept nodding forward on his thick neck, and he had to shake it before he could lift it again.

"Listen. Don't you remember the fairy tales?"

The basket of stones beside the bed with the rubber sheet. Granny and Red. The missing wolves and woodsmen. The overflowing well. It all made sense.

When he was a cub, his mother had terrified him and his siblings with tales of the evil old Granny who used to send a pretty young girl out alone into the woods to lure wolves back to her home with promises of roast chicken and stuffed rabbit. But when they got to the house, the food was drugged and the innocent wolf would fall asleep. Then the evil Granny would bring the wolf to bed, but not to sleep. Instead, she'd slice his belly open to spill out all the blood, roast chicken and stuffed rabbit, and fill him up with rocks instead. She'd sew him back up and as soon as the poor groggy wolf woke, she'd scream until a woodsman came to save her, chasing the wolf into a river, where he'd sink under the weight of the rocks in his stomach.

"Finish him, Woodie, and we'll be together, like I promised," rasped Granny, unable to keep up Red's voice.

"Sure, Red," said Woodie.

"Red? This is Granny!" said Wolf.

"It's Red."

"It's Granny," said Wolf. "And if you're wondering where all your 'noble brothers' are, they're not in the city. They're outside in Granny's well together with the wolves, their bellies full of the rocks she sewed into them."

"You dummy, that's just a... fairy tale. And... the Granny only... did it to wolves. The woodsmen were the... heroes! Right... Red?" His voice was slurred, although he'd only had one glass of wine. "Red?"

"Sure," said Granny.

"You don't sound sure, Granny," said Wolf. "Having second thoughts about hooking up with this guy and dealing with his questions for the rest of your life?"

"Die, Wolf!" screamed Granny. "Cut him, you moron!" she said to Woodie, who was blinking slowly in their general direction.

"Let me guess, it's the 'til death do us part' bit of the wedding ceremony you're most looking forward to?" Wolf asked her.

Woodie swayed but stayed standing, listening to them both. "You don't love me, Red?" Behind his coke-bottle glasses, his eyes had already closed.

"This is Granny!" said Wolf. "Jee-zus!"

"I'm Granny, you moron!" said Granny.

"Then where's Red?" asked Woodie.

"I think she's in the cupboard. And she's in trouble, Woodie. We all are." Wolf edged towards the cupboard, which is where the tapping sound he'd heard all evening was coming from.

"She's safe," said Granny. "Don't worry about Red. Everybody wants Red. Everybody loves Red."

"I love you, Re… Granny?" said Woodie.

"You're worse than he is," spat Granny at him. "At least a wolf is only doing what a wolf does. You and your 'Purist' crap. You make me sick. Red's too good for either of you."

Wolf took a calculated risk and let Granny go, and she advanced on Woodie, berating him. With them distracted, Wolf peered through the slats of the wardrobe. Even in the dark, he recognised Red's big, beautiful brown eyes.

Suddenly, he felt a lot braver. It didn't much matter what happened next, as long as Red was safe. He edged the door of the cupboard open a bit and snaked a paw inside. He felt the ropes she'd been tied up with, then extended his claws and felt her lean into them, using them to cut through her bonds. One rope snapped, followed by another.

"What's wrong with Purism?" said Woodie. "I thought you were all in favour."

"Of course you did! Too blind to see what's really going on. Too blind to see what Red really is." Granny had paced around the bed, forcing Woodie to crawl back over it to retreat from her anger. She dug an enormous pair of scissors out of the basket with the stones.

Wolf prepared to pounce, waiting to see which of them he'd need to take care of, though it didn't look like Woodie knew what was going on. Any minute now he was going to let Granny cut him out of sheer, misguided love for her.

"I raised Red. She's mine, I'm going to keep her away from all of you!" Wolf's fur bristled as Granny suddenly turned and raked him with eyes dazed with hate. "It's your fault, Wolf. Your kind all talk so smoothly. One of your kind had my daughter convinced it was love! My daughter and a wolf! That's not how I raised her, to lie with filthy animals. I took care of him, but she never recovered after he was gone. She just faded away. So when Red was born, I looked after her. She'll never be pure, but she's mine, and no one else is going to have her."

"Not pure?" Woodie was holding himself up with difficulty, draped against the wall, his large head resting on his arm. As soon as he dropped, Granny was going to slice him. She was only talking until he fell asleep. The wine had been drugged. If Wolf had drunk it, he'd be unconscious by now. Only the woodcutter's bulk kept him still awake.

"She's half-human, half-wolf!" said Granny. That's when Woodie collapsed. Like a felled tree, he crashed lengthwise onto the bed. Granny dived at him and Wolf jumped, grabbing the scissors as she raised them over her head to strike.

"No, Granny!" shouted Red, springing out of the cupboard.

"Run, Red!" shouted Wolf. "Get help!"

"Not a chance!" said Red. "We both know how that ends: 'Wolf Slain During Granny Attack!'"

Wolf turned to her, even as he struggled with Granny, who was trying to buck him off. She was more beautiful than ever. Those big brown eyes, that pale skin, those pink lips. And now, he also saw something else. The reason she'd always worn that hood, never left home without it.

"Don't look at me!" she said.

With Granny wearing her clothes, Red was bare-headed for the first time. She tried to cover herself with her hands, but it was too late. Sticking out of the top of her head, soft, furry and pricked straight up, were two of the cutest ears Wolf had ever seen. The reason she "wasn't pure," the reason Granny hated wolves and Purists so much.

Wolf could only stare. "You're beautiful, Red."

When the police drained the well, they found the bodies of all the missing wolves and woodsmen, going back for years.

Wolf and Red had tried to talk Granny down, while Woodie went for help—Red wrote everything down for him, so he only had to hand the note to the police—but in the confusion Granny had managed to grab the wine bottle and down it all in one go, overdosing on the drug in it. Her old heart had stopped before the police turned up.

Things could never go back to the way they were, but it seemed to Wolf that the forest shone brighter after that storm. The leaves were greener, the flowers lusher and brighter, and if there were still people who talked about Purism, Red and Wolf didn't care.

After several weeks, the furore died down and after several more, they felt comfortable around each other again. It helped that Woodie had decided to try his luck in the city. He said he didn't understand the forest anymore.

September had almost passed before they kissed. Red's teeth were as small, and her breath was as hot and sweet as Wolf remembered, but she never wore her hood again, and her hair and her furry ears were the colour of the autumn leaves around them.

Dead Fox Masks

This is a straight-up horror story, because I wanted to write something scary. If you like it, then let me know. As you'll see, there's plenty of scope to turn this into something much bigger. Hollywood: for the film version, I'll be insisting on old-school prosthetics, rather than CGI for the special effects, okay?

I trust the old man who pilots the boat, because he's not wearing a uniform, unlike the doctors and soldiers on the quay. He's unfazed by all the fuss. It's easy to imagine that the world could end around him, and he'd still be sailing this diesel-stinking tub.

He checks I'm onboard, then busies himself with the dials set into the boat's carbon-fibre dashboard. I almost puke from nerves when the soldiers drop to their knees to sight down their gun barrels after us, making sure we leave. The old man just twists a key, sending tremors through the deck as the motor sputters into life, en route to Singer Island, where the Callers go.

"What's it really like?" I ask, as the boat enters the choppy waters of the open sea. He pauses before he answers, long enough for me to wonder if I should have called him "Captain."

"Killer cure," he says, the words chewed up by his rough voice and guttural accent.

I feel better to hear him say it. I'll be fine. My eyes close. I haven't slept in four days, not since they found out I was a Caller.

"No sleeping," he says.

I can sleep on the island. That's the whole point. The doctors say hard work is the best cure. I'll have the whole place to myself, nothing to think about or upset me. No coffee, no tea, no alcohol, no cigarettes. No phone reception, no internet, no radio. There's a larder full of tinned soups and stews for the cold weather. In summer, the island is one big farm with fields of potatoes and carrots. Berries. Apple trees. I can have anything I want, as long as I harvest it myself. Fresh water from my own well with a bucket on a hand-cranked rope. Plenty of hard work, so I sleep too deeply for the dreams to find me. So nothing gets Called, and no one gets hurt. A killer cure. I'll be fine once my arms get used to the manual labour. It'll be like boot camp. I'll come back ripped.

———

It's not working. I spend the first few days clearing out the cottage from whatever Caller was here before me. It stinks of mouldy vegetables and shrivelled blue-powdered fruits. There are so many it takes forever to dump it all outside, dust the mould away. But every muscle aches from the exercise, waking me whenever I nod off.

Whoever was there must have left in a hurry, because they'd left the door open and the lights on. I imagine them working, working, working to tire themselves out, then suddenly hearing the ship's horn and racing to the boat to go back to civilisation. The thought keeps me going.

Once I clear out the rotten food, I start harvesting my own. Those first few days, my muscles are so sore I think I'll go home an invalid. But I've got used to it now, and the dreams are back. I'm still Calling.

It started after the Rift appeared, that hole which splits the sky, glaring white light at night and black light during the day. People say the dreams start when you look into it too long. I swear I didn't. The dreams started all by themselves.

And when I dream, I Call, pulling creatures out of whatever Hell the Rift opens onto. There was chaos at first when the creatures were Called into the world. Once they pull themselves into our world through the dreams of Callers they kill everyone, burn and destroy everything they find. They kill almost everyone. Sometimes they take people back through the Rift with them, human flesh melting and transforming as it passes through the hole in the sky.

I'm lucky. There are no more summary executions now. There's a chance of rehabilitation on Singer's Island.

———

Twenty tall, thin figures march out of the sea. Beetles, taller than a human, and walking upright on their hind legs. Ticking towards me with stop-motion jerkiness, sloughing water and seaweed.

Under the light of the Rift, their black carapaces have the rainbow gleam of petrol. They're a funeral procession searching for a corpse. Looking for me, while pretending otherwise.

Forelegs clutch spears and jagged swords, the claws of their middle legs tap out a marching rhythm on their abdomens. With every step, their antennae and the feeler hairs on their limbs and down their backs shake and twitch, scenting me.

They're hunters and they're camouflaged, all wearing the same mask: the hollowed out head of a skinned fox. Its dead eyes stare forward, the fur is bedraggled and greenish. The lifeless mouth is frozen open in a snarl. But the masks aren't big enough and don't hide their cruel mandibles, or their unblinking compound eyes, which they keep fixed straight ahead as they approach. Pretending it'll only be chance when they find me.

In the dream, I'm in my bed, but also hovering over them. They sense me, but pretend they can't. I know they are coming to kill me, but pretend I don't. It's only that stupid pretence which keeps me alive. If we shatter the pretence, the game is over. If I panic, if I move, if I should look directly at them, then they win, and whatever they do to me will be a thousand times worse than simple death.

I suppose that if they break the rules first, then I win, but I have a feeling that's not going to happen. So I choke back my panic, freeze my trembling limbs and keep my eyes fixed on the ground near their feet as they approach my helpless body, so I can see them without acknowledging they're there. Getting closer every night.

I wear myself out with work. The skin on my hands cracks in different places every day. The air is so fresh, it burns my nostrils. Sometimes I doze for an hour in the fields. Never in my bed, they know where I sleep. I need to work harder, harder, like the doctor said. I'm not tired enough, is all.

It's a killer cure. The old man said so.

I fetch water from the well, boil it on a fire I feed with the logs I've chopped. When I open the door to the larder, the potatoes I've harvested tumble out, trying to escape the burst and spoiled blackberries lying on them. But I'm not tired enough. I'll call the monsters if I sleep. Instead I go to the orchard to pluck apples, then dump the full baskets outside so the apples can stare blank-eyed into the Rift. I have no appetite.

My head feels funny. The lack of company, perhaps. It'd be nice to have someone to talk to, to pass the long nights. Instead, I work in the fields, only coming home to drink water, careful to switch the light on first, so the dark doesn't tempt me into staying. The Rift shines bright, but doesn't illuminate anything.

The silence in my ears changes texture, and I know they've arrived, making their clockwork way up from the beach. It's too late to hide, and if I'm dreaming, I don't know how to wake up.

I don't think I'm asleep. Perhaps they've made it all the way through to our world, and the Rift's logic applies: I'll live so long as I can stay silent and motionless.

The light in the cottage pins me in the kitchen window. Any movement I make would be clearly visible. They come closer than they've ever come before, silent but for the tapping of their claws on their hard bellies. When they reach the cottage, they spread out and circle it.

They keep their fox masks pointed away, but their bulging insect eyes are already feeding on me, choosing the best bits. Their feelers twitch in anticipation of digging through my soft flesh.

I stare at a point on the ground, make no sign that I see them marching past my window. One of them is always in view as they march around the cottage, so I have no chance to move. Their feet swish through the coarse grass outside. They're so close that the blades of their weapons scrape against the walls of my cottage.

Their eyes stare directly at me now. They must have twisted their long necks while out of my sight.

That's allowed, because I didn't see them do it. The fox heads, still bloody and dripping seawater, stare over my shoulder and my watering eyes are fixed on a safe patch of ground, which I pretend interests me more than the black, armoured legs that keep flashing past, getting in the way.

Let them stare all they want. I can see the cottage's door from the corner of my eye, so they can't get in without me seeing them, without giving the game away. Staring at nothing is easy. I'm going to make it.

I'll be fine. The old man said so. Then the light above me goes off.

I turn to run, but of course I'm surrounded, and the door is already squealing open.

In the sudden darkness, I'm blind, so I stay motionless. I don't know whether I'm awake or asleep, but it doesn't matter. The rules of the Rift still apply.

If I don't move and don't make a sound, and don't look at them, they can't touch me. Shadows move, and the room feels alive with their presence. But it's deathly quiet as they wait for me to give myself away. I keep my eyes on the ground at my feet.

I can't see you, I think as loud as I can. *Can't hear you. I can't* smell *you*, and the thought falters, because I can.

Once the light comes back on, everything will be fine.

It's a killer cure. Nothing to worry about.

Unless.

Unless it was "kill or cure."

I try to swallow, but my throat is so dry that I hear the rasping of it as the musky scent of wet fur presses ever deeper into my lungs. I choke on it, cough, and the cold snout of a dead fox touches my face. My body goes limp, but sharp claws snatch my arms and legs. I wait for them to disembowel me, hack my limbs off, but the nightmare isn't over yet.

The claws pluck me off the ground.

They're taking me to the Rift.

Goes Without Saying

We're due to move countries for work this year. I started this fantasy story around the time I was researching Greece as a possible destination.
Having found out how it ends, I'm sure that if we ever end up there, I'll be mostly relieved if the donkeys in Athens can't talk.
But maybe just a little disappointed, too.

———

It was getting dark as I headed back towards my hotel in Kolonaki, but I didn't worry. Except for the anarchists, Athens is a safe place to go for a walk, even at night. As long as you watch out for the donkeys.

"Good evening, my friend."

I turned to see who had hailed me. A donkey grinned from an alleyway. I didn't respond, but he fell into step beside me, anyway.

I've always liked donkeys, when I've seen them on television or whatever, but I didn't like this one. A black patch of hair in the middle of his muzzle gave him an unfortunate Hitler moustache.

He would have been ugly, anyway. He was scrawny, with stringy muscles along his neck, pressing against his skin like worms under the patchy hair. A bite was missing from one of his ears. And he stank as though he slept in his own filth. Worst of all, though, was his expression.

His head hung low, twisting away to watch me from the corner of his eye, but with a sly grin twitching at his mouth. His cheek trembled with the effort of disguising it. He made me think of an orange paperback of *Aesop's Fables* I had owned as a child, where smug animals always "won" against the less clever.

He definitely had a Hitler moustache, rather than a Chaplin one; there was nothing funny about him. Outside the tourist areas, there weren't many cafes, and we were alone together on the dark, empty street.

"American?" he asked.

I ignored him.

"Rude," he said, but his cheek twitched. He hadn't expected to catch me out so easily.

I often got asked if I was American when I wore my camera strapped around my neck, as I did now.

When I left it at the hotel, the locals guessed (correctly) that I was English, instead. I enjoyed the innocent deception. It was like wearing a disguise.

I kept to the path, that narrow strip of pavement between the buildings and the row of parked cars. It wasn't wide enough for the donkey, whose swollen belly swung underneath him between spidery legs. He clacked along on the road. Not a horse's "clip, clop," because a street donkey didn't wear horseshoes. More like a dog's nails on a hardwood floor. Louder, of course.

"You go to the Acropolis?"

It was amazing how well everyone here spoke English, though I still sometimes struggled when the thick Greek accent twisted familiar sounds into unfamiliar shapes. I wouldn't have answered him in any case, but as it happened I couldn't, because I didn't know if he was asking if I had already been, or if I planned to go later. I was sure he would have some sort of "special offer" if I said yes.

"Because I can smell it." He hurried—clack, clack, clack, clack, clack, clack—to overtake me on the road. Without looking directly at me—grinning towards my chin—he gave me a complicit look. "They won't let you back in the hotel like that."

We had come to an alleyway, and I hurried to cross the road, hoping that would be the end of it. I glanced into the alley to check for cars and mopeds, and movement caught my eye.

The dark made it hard to see, but it looked like a tiny knot of donkeys foraging along the wall. Or perhaps stuck in a doorway, all pushing to get through first, and getting more jammed in the process. One donkey stood apart, on guard. The knot moved again, and a man stood up out of the mess of bodies.

All I could really see were two gleaming eyes. He must have been dark-skinned, for he was barely discernable in the shadows, other than where his skin glistened wetly in the moonlight to suggest ridges and bumps. Almost like muscles rather than skin. He froze when he noticed me, which in turn alerted the guard donkey, who moved in my direction.

My donkey shouted something and the guard donkey turned back. A moment later, the group disappeared into the gloom. Four pale donkeys.

That's two pairs, because donkeys mate up, don't they? There was no sign of a man.

"I can get rid of it for you," said my donkey, when we were alone again. "It must be heavy, carrying it with two legs."

I walked on, wondering how much further the hotel was. Going back was always harder, because it's uphill.

I decided to call the donkey Charlie, rather than Adolf, in my head, after all. I wanted to turn him into a figure of ridicule, rather than of fear. It didn't look like he was going to give up, though he'd surely have found easier marks elsewhere.

Kolonaki is one of Athens' better neighbourhoods, but the narrow streets are just as choked as everywhere else. Charlie continued to trot along the road, shooting glances at me between the parked cars, while I got more and more out of breath. It would be easiest to give him some money, and then I could enjoy the walk home, but I refused to give in to his bullying. And I couldn't thank him for scaring away the others, if that was what he expected, because the guidebooks were very clear that engaging a donkey in conversation was one of the worst things a tourist could do. Of course, it also said they generally lost interest fairly quickly.

I could conjure up the exact page in my mind. My sister had highlighted the passage in yellow (and bent back the edge of the page, which ruined the book).

> "… while wolves mate for life to take better care of their young, donkeys bond to keep arguing with each other. Greek donkeys, in particular, are notorious for their willingness to debate anything. They are tenacious in arguing their point, and aggressive when logical errors make their argument indefensible. It is best to completely avoid any conversation with a donkey while on holidays.
> "It goes without saying that you should never, under any circumstances, touch a donkey!"

"What would your sister say if you arrived back like that?" My chin itched from all the subtext his sly glances kept throwing at it. It was just a trick. He couldn't know that I had a sister. He wanted to surprise a response out of me. After all, he had got it wrong about me being an American.

I wondered about the warning not to touch donkeys. It was hard to imagine anyone stroking Charlie. The missing patches of hair on his pelt were doubtless a result of age and hard living, rather than from petting. What bits he still possessed were knotted and stood in dusty tufts. I wondered what it would be like to touch him. Not that I wanted to.

We passed another alleyway, and I crossed the road without looking, the image of a man's red, raw face rising in front of me. Some people did touch donkeys, after all.

I'd been on the go since that morning, and my throat was painfully dry. I had drunk nothing since visiting the Acropolis that morning. Before everything had gone wrong.

"We can go in here," said Charlie.

To our left, a set of narrow overgrown steps between two houses wound their way up the hill, into a wooded area. He stopped to wait for me to go in.

Instead, I took the opportunity to cross the road again into another side street. It would take me away from my hotel, but people moved about in the dim light of sleepy bars and cafes and I wanted company more than anything else at that moment. As I hurried away from Charlie, the waxy smell of vegetation, the wood polish scent of the ubiquitous olive trees, and the earthy aroma of a freshly watered garden greeted me. I'd been with the donkey so long, I'd got used to his smell from breathing it in.

I didn't want him following me. I certainly didn't want him to find out where I was staying in case he made a fuss. The sight of the man and the donkeys in the alleyway wasn't such an uncommon sight as you might think, and I would hate for the receptionist to think I was that kind of tourist.

Especially if it meant she discreetly turned a blind eye to Charlie's presence in the belief that I was trying to sneak him up to my room. And when I checked out, I'd have to leave her a good tip for that "favour!"

"Good idea," he said, having caught up to me, as I stood outside the first bar, examining the menu on the wall, like a normal tourist. "Have a drink first, eh?"

But my luck was turning. Even as he pushed his face forward to give me his creepy grin, I noticed that the bar's entrance was set down half a dozen steps from the road, which would make it difficult for him to follow me.

It was impossible to read the menu, as the only light came from a red lantern hanging on the far side of the entrance. It painted the whitewashed walls a liverish purple and, after all, it didn't really matter; I just wanted to get away. I hoped it was a bar and not a brothel, with the red light. But as long as it had human girls, I didn't care. If they insisted, I could pay for an hour without being obliged to *do* anything. My heart actually lightened at the thought that I could sit in peace for an hour and finally fill out my holiday postcards. I had a pocket full of them as I collected them wherever I went, usually without ever sending them. It would give my family a shock when one turned up this time!

I pushed through the door into a basement. There was a Formica counter with bottles arranged on shelves around a curtained doorway behind it. Rickety tables and chairs lined the walls, while the middle of the floor was packed earth and empty. Perhaps there'd be music and dancing later. A man peered from behind the curtain and jerked a thumb to one corner, indicating another curtained doorway. I assumed it led to the more comfortable dining area, but it was just an alcove, with a crushed velvet couch against the back wall, and a mat on the near side of a small table.

"I think you've been here before, my friend," said the donkey. He stood right behind me, his head low to the ground and so close that my leg almost brushed against his awful "moustache" when I turned. The heat of his bulk radiated against my hand. His hair looked soft in the dim light, and he gave me that awful grin. I chose a table in the front room instead and took out my postcards, waiting for the barman to serve me and kick the donkey out. As I pulled my cards out, their paper bag crinkled.

"You're going to write on the back?" asked Charlie. He snickered.

Where was the barman?

"Maybe look at the front first."

He was infuriating. I had been about to look at the front, to decide which ones I would send to my mother, which to my sister, but now I couldn't, or it would look like I was heeding his suggestion, when I needed to ignore him.

I cleared my throat to summon the barman, and Charlie backed away until he hovered behind me, his head palpably close to my elbow. Then I counted to thirty and turned the postcards over.

The Parthenon at the Acropolis, two more cards with views of the sunrise from there.

A fishing boat painted with blue and white circles that ward off the evil eye.

A beach.

A large white building against a blue background of sea and clear sky. The building looked like a cross between a windmill and a Disney castle.

And on all of them, arms wrapped around each other, were my mother, my sister and my father.

I turned on my phone's flashlight to make sure. I hadn't seen my father since he had disappeared silently one day when I was nine years old. The happy family smiled between the Parthenon's columns, waved from a beach towel on the sand, leaned together in the narrow boat. My father's hair was greyer than I remembered, his paunch bigger, but it was definitely him.

My face burned with shame. There wasn't a single photo of me, and they'd never mentioned being to Greece, not even when I'd told them where I was going on holiday.

———

I gave up on getting a drink.

Outside, the night was too warm. I'd been out all day, sweating after the morning's excitement, and I probably stank. Charlie followed me, anyway.

I wanted to punch someone, so I kept my hands in my pockets. It would still count as touching, wouldn't it? If I punched him for showing me the postcards?

Not that it mattered. Nothing seemed to matter at that moment. Not if my father was alive, kept from me by my mother and sister.

Mind you, I had already touched a donkey that morning. And paid dearly for it, too. What would it matter if I touched another one?

"I can take it off you," murmured Charlie. When I looked around, I realised I was lost. Luckily, we were somewhere where our "odd couple" act didn't stick out too much. I could see at least three other worried men being herded along by grinning donkeys. Charlie whistled to one of them across the street, and they broke into a torrent of lightning-fast Greek.

I examined the other donkey's man. He looked lost and lonely, and I pitied him. Then we moved on, and that's when I made the decision. If I went on like this much longer, I would become as lost as the other man.

"Here," I said. I held out a twenty euro note. "It's yours, if you can tell me how to get back to the Hotel Zafeiri."

Charlie looked straight at me for the first time that night, his eyes boring into mine, his nostrils flaring. When he spoke, his teeth were yellow, and a few were missing, but they looked sharp and tough.

"Give it to me," he said.

"I'm not allowed to touch donkeys."

"No," he agreed. "But you did."

I threw the money at him and ran.

It felt like I'd been running all day.

"This way," he called behind me.

I ignored him.

"You come with me."

Question or statement? I disappeared around the corner. Without his grin and sneaky eyes plastered all over me, it was like the sudden balm of shade after hours of relentless sun. If he followed me, I would call the police. My sister had typed the number into my dual-SIM phone, warning me it was only for emergencies. I didn't fancy a brush with the Greek police, though it was unlikely they knew who I was. Perhaps Charlie had spotted me straight away when I passed his alleyway. He'd been stringing me along, laughing at me, until it was time to tell me what he really wanted. Of course, he wouldn't take a measly twenty euros to keep quiet about what he knew. I was gladder than ever that I hadn't gone straight to my hotel. He'd have led everyone straight there.

Then I remembered I'd just told him the hotel's name.

———

I take two holidays by myself every year. It's nice to get away, and I have a well-paid job, and no family. It feels less lonely when you're on your own in a foreign country, because *of course* you don't know anyone there, and you can cheer yourself up with the thought that you'll soon be home again.

Or buy yourself postcards and delude yourself you'll keep in touch that way.

I never usually get up in time to see the sunrise when I'm on holidays, but that morning I'd got to the Acropolis early. Barely half a dozen tour buses grazed in the carpark, and the day's warm air hadn't yet dried out. There weren't any donkeys around.

At the time, I hadn't even noticed, but looking back, that's the most obvious thing. If I was thinking about anything, I was thinking about what I'd have for lunch, as the Hotel Zafeiri does a particularly light continental breakfast. The point is, I wasn't thinking about donkeys at all.

I wandered around the ruins, took some photos, then wandered over to the edge of the hill the whole Acropolis squats on. There's an excellent view of Athens from there. I took a few photos of that, then wandered down the hill to the kiosk to buy some postcards and a bottle of water. I almost left, but I'd only spent about twenty minutes at the Acropolis and didn't have anything else planned before lunch, as I'd been expecting it to be bigger. So, I went back up and sat under one of the few trees that offered shade.

I'd already photographed everything, so I just day-dreamed and drank water. A donkey nosed around on the far side of the Parthenon ruins, keeping well away from the arriving tourists. I found I preferred watching her to looking at the ruins. They were only bloody stones, after all.

I sat there quite happily for a while. In fact, I watched her long enough to have to move position twice to stay in the tree's shade.

The donkey paid me no attention, and I wasn't doing anything, just looking. She ambled around, picking at grass, following the paltry shadow the hill's low wall offered. She looked exhausted, but so alive.

In case you've never been there, it's stark. There's the tree I was sitting under, two other trees (one of which is historically important, and both of which are roped off), and the rest of it is flat, dry, old stone. Seeing an actual living creature up there made it special. Of course, I was surrounded by tourists, but they hardly counted.

This was a Greek donkey, wandering around the ruins of Greek civilisation. She brought the whole place to life. Her hair was black-brown, and she had long ears which twitched as she listened to the movements of the people around her. Her muzzle was dainty, and her eyes were brown when her gaze met mine. I looked away, then looked back. She had moved further, but kept an eye on me, probably because I was the closest human. I offered her my water, but she took a step back, her eyes widening. So, I left the bottle on the ground and moved away, took a few more shots of the Parthenon, to give her a chance to drink.

It was time to go, and I wandered slowly down the hill, having *felt* something for once, rather than just doing my duty as a conscientious tourist. It was getting on for midday by now, and the road was deserted, yet I didn't hear her hooves until she had caught up to me.

She held the bottle carefully in her mouth so the water wouldn't spill. "Thank you," she said, pronouncing the words exactly.

I nodded and took my bottle back.

Her wet muzzle shone, and the skin quivered around her nostrils like exquisite leather. I was careful not to touch her, but we stood very close and she smelled like a fresh hotel pillow. We trotted along together-but-not-together.

A lump like warm caramel loosened in my chest. I was at peace and proud to have her walking by my side. There was only a little water left in the bottle. She refused when I offered it to her, so I drank it.

I kept the water in my mouth for a long moment, wondering if I only imagined that it tasted sweeter from having come from her lips.

The sun kept piling on the heat as we walked the winding route away from the ruins, and her proximity was making me giddy. She kept "mmm-ing," as if she wanted to speak, but couldn't work up the courage.

So I spoke. "I need to sit down," I said, making for some trees lining the path. It was infernally hot.

She came with me, and we sat between spiky bushes with no blooms.

Would you believe me if I told you I don't know what happened next, or how it happened?

If someone is to blame, then blame me, of course, but we fell into each other, our limbs tangling together, and her mouth was soft and her tongue was hot and her hair, oh God, the hair of her cheeks and flanks! Judge if you like, but I'd never been so happy before, and she felt the same. She whispered in my ear, lapsing into Greek, so I didn't understand the words, but under them thumped the painful joy of a heart so full it might burst.

I'd never done anything like that before, and in the open, too. We lay together, her coat scratching my upper arm, alone in the warm afternoon. I couldn't get enough of the cross that ran the length of her spine, and plunged my fingers through its soft-coarse hair. She sighed contentedly. We dozed.

I woke in pain as she staggered to her feet. She had used her jaw to push herself up and, as it had been resting on my arm, the sudden pinch startled me. Greeks with serious, lined faces and thick noses, all dressed either in black or white, surrounded us.

I jumped up, grabbing my clothes and camera strap in one arm, and putting out my other arm in front of my donkey to keep her safe behind me.

A man shouted, and she shouted back, while the crowd eyed us. I tried to cover myself with my balled-up clothes, then someone threw a rock, and then they were all throwing rocks. My donkey—*my donkey!*—bleated in pain as a rock thumped into her neck.

We ran, pursued by the mob. Rocks hit me all over, twice on my head, crunching my teeth painfully together, and once in my side, which almost brought me down as the ache kept expanding, shrinking the amount of air my burning lungs were able to suck in. We kept going over the hard, treacherous ground, littered with brittle twigs and sharp stones which ripped at the soul of my feet. We zigzagged through the trees, fell down a slope—which was the most terrifying thing that had ever happened to me: not knowing if I was going to break every bone in my body, smash my brains out at the bottom, or just be knocked unconscious for the mob to catch up and lynch—and they kept coming.

When we made it to the bottom of the hill, I tried to grab hold of her so we wouldn't get separated. We dodged across the road to a cacophony of brakes and horns, and I turned left, aiming for a narrow alley, which seemed familiar, and she went right.

In the time it took for me to realise I had lost her, the mob had reached the bottom of the hill, too. I hid in a souvenir shop, fumbling note after note from my wallet into the outstretched hand of the shopkeeper as they swarmed down the street.

As soon as I had pulled my clothes on, I doubled back. But she was gone, having disappeared before we could say anything important to one another.

———

Charlie found me sitting on a wall, looking through the postcards.

"Hello, USA," he said.

"I'm English." I didn't care about the postcards anymore, or the people on them. Charlie knew what I had done, and he'd want his pound of flesh. I hadn't paid for my crime, after all. Being attacked was part of it. Losing my donkey was part of it. But that was atonement. I still needed to be punished.

"I know that," said Charlie. "I always call the English 'Americans.' Like I always greet the Japanese with '*ni hao*.'" He stood in front of me, close enough for his breath to bend the postcards. I left them on the wall. "You shouldn't have done it."

He wasn't grinning at me, and he wasn't giving me a sly look. He was so ugly, I would have felt bad for him if it wasn't for that moustache. I could hardly blame him for being born with such an unlucky marking, but it was truly hideous.

"Get used to it," he said. "You knew it was wrong to touch her."

"I love her."

"Fine, but a rule's a rule."

"Can't you at least tell me where she is?"

"Don't worry, I'll help you. This is a win-win situation, my friend."

I hesitated.

"Or stay where you are and talk to the police." He moved away as a slow patrol car rolled in our direction. I looked at the windows of the houses around us. All the curtains were drawn and the lights off, but I knew I was being observed by serious thick-nosed people, watching to make sure I followed the rules. In the dark, all of them were dressed in black.

———

I recognised where we were. It was close to my hotel. A dark narrow staircase led up the hill, set between two houses.

"We do it here," he said.

I remembered the man and the group of donkeys.

"Are you a… man or a woman?" I asked, in case that made a difference.

"I'm a donkey." He scratched his flanks against the wall of one of the houses, then rolled on the ground. "Help me."

I gave him my hand and pulled him up. The skin hung soft and loose around his thin legs, as though it wasn't really his. I squeezed it and when he took a neat step backwards, the whole thing came off.

Then it was my turn, and I scratched against the walls and rolled on the pavement, but my skin was stuck. Charlie couldn't help, because he was truly naked, with hands of bloody and wet muscle. But after squirming a while longer on the ground, then using the edge of the steps to loosen up a flap of skin beside my mouth, it came off, and we swapped.

It was comfortable once I had it on, though there was a queasy moment when the realisation hit me that I would be putting on someone else's skin (I didn't know *where* he'd been). That passed as the skin shifted and tightened to fit.

Charlie stood looking at his arms and legs, twisting them and feeling them move. Seen from outside, I really wasn't such a catch. I hoped he'd be happy and laughed.

"What?"

"You look funny up on two legs," I said.

He spat and put my clothes on, then swore when he saw how empty my wallet was.

"What now?" I asked.

But he was already disappearing up the steps, without even saying goodbye, or telling me where to go next. He ran too fast for me to catch him, had I wanted to.

Which I didn't.

I made my way slowly back to the Acropolis to find her.

Schrödinger's Fault

Science fiction! I don't write a lot of sci-fi, but I'm happy with this one.
I read Douglas Adams's Dirk Gently's Holistic Detective Agency *soon after it first came out, so have had Schrödinger's cat stuck in my head for most of my life. Now that I have finally written a story about it, I can hopefully let it go.*
Dead or alive, as they say.

It was Schrödinger's fault.

Wait, that's not fair.

It was his idea, but he only ever intended it as a thought experiment. You couldn't actually do it.

Not without a cat.

Luckily, our neighbour, Mrs Quigley, has… or should that be had? a cat.

And it wasn't Martin's fault. He was only being Martin.

You certainly couldn't blame the cat.

Which means it must have been my fault for not firmly putting my foot down when Martin started preparing the shed for the experiment. Three days we were going to have to spend in there.

"She's alive?" I asked, as Martin opened up the box three days later. I'd been dreading the prospect of finding poor Queenie dead.

"Alive-ish," said Martin.

He stood over the foldable table in the centre of our shed. A single naked lightbulb glared down on his fine brown hair as he examined the cat. I sat on a camping chair close to the locked door, burrowing deeper into my coat, scarf and thick woollen socks, although the shed was warm enough after three days of body heat and no fresh air. I just wanted to distance myself from the experiment.

Too little, too late, of course.

Eventually, I looked over to see what he meant. In order to guarantee the purity of the experiment, Martin had insisted we lock ourselves in the shed, covering the windows and even blocking the gaps under the door and keyhole, so that the results wouldn't be influenced by anything other than our observation. I had a headache, and the air was hot, sticky with our combined breath and beyond stale despite the air fresheners around the covered bucket in the corner. If I wanted to get out of the shed—which I did—I'd have to look.

"She's moving," I said.

"Yes," said Martin, but he didn't sound convinced. Queenie, an old, tiger-striped red cat with yellow eyes, pink bum, and terrible breath, had been in the closed-up box for the last three days.

For science.

Martin had just let her out, and she held no apparent grudge, massaging the table with all four paws while arching her back to rub against Martin's outstretched hand.

"Well, that's good enough for me." I stood up, delighted that we'd all survived.

"But look!" said Martin.

So I took a closer look. We'd camped in a tent at the back of the shed, and I'd have to go past him anyway to get the shed's key from his rucksack. I was going to wash away my headache with the biggest glass of red wine I could find as soon as I got back in the house.

Queenie wasn't pushing herself against Martin's hands, she was pushing herself *through* Martin's hands. Her body was *there*, but transparent like swirling cigar smoke.

"She's a ghost!" I said.

"Maybe," said Martin.

He furrowed his brow as he stared at Queenie and then into the box she'd spent three days in, trying to work out what this meant.

I felt terrible for Queenie, though she seemed happy enough. How would I face Mrs Quigley after this? Martin was the physicist, but as I understood it, Schrödinger had come up with this "experiment" to demonstrate a problem with the Copenhagen interpretation of quantum mechanics. Basically, if you put a cat in a box with a poison pellet in such a way that the poison may or may not kill the cat, then the cat remains dead and alive until some outside observer opens the box to check which.

Ridiculous.

And yet…

After allowing him to lock me inside a cramped box of a shed for my bank holiday weekend, I would be back teaching *To Kill A Mockingbird* tomorrow, trying to explain to fourteen-year-olds who'd grown up with cyber-bullying, catfishing and fake news, why Atticus thought the Boo Radley game was such a big deal. I needed that wine.

Still, perhaps we had discovered something. "So, have we done it?" I asked.

"No," said Martin. He bit his lip, and I followed his glance into the box. Curled up on the bottom of it was another transparent tiger-striped red cat. This one wasn't moving. *Poor Queenie!* The poison pellet was there too, but tears pricked at my eyes, blurring my vision, so I couldn't see if it had gone off or not. I went to stroke the body, then pulled my fingers back before they sank into it.

"So Queenie is dead *and* alive." I didn't feel triumph at proving the Copenhagen interpretation worked, just sad that we'd killed Queenie.

Possibly twice.

"She can't be," said Martin, his eyes flicking from one version of the cat to the other. "Once the experiment ends, she must be dead or alive."

"I'm not staying in this bloody shed any longer!"

"Once the experiment ends..." Martin spoke as if to himself, thinking it out. Sweat beaded on his forehead, glistening under the merciless interrogation of the dangling light bulb over his head. "I think she's still part of it." His voice gave me goosebumps.

"I'm not staying," I said, but didn't move. I had no idea what would happen if the experiment was interrupted, but was sure it'd be bad. Instead, I leaned over Queenie's box to get a better look at the poison pellet. We had locked ourselves in, *sealed ourselves in*, so nothing from outside could disturb the experiment.

Perhaps not even fresh air.

"*We're* not dead. Are we?" I felt stupid for asking.

"Maybe." Martin waved his hand through Queenie's silhouette, and my stomach churned. "We're alive too, though. At least until the experiment is over."

But if we were in the experiment, that would mean someone else was observing us, despite the blocked doors and windows.

That's when I saw you. You. Yes, you! You reading this. Hey! Can't you hear me? Stop reading! Please! Stop, before it's too late!

Don't you get it?

This is the experiment. And even if Martin and I have died, we're still alive, too. We can live in here as long as the experiment continues. But as soon as you read the final word, we'll—

The Last Top Hat I
Ever Saw

On the tram to Berlin's Hauptbahnhof last year, I saw a man carrying a classy-looking tan leather suitcase. It looked very heavy. This creepy horror tale reveals the only possible thing that could have been inside.
If he reads this, would the gentleman concerned please get in touch to let me know he's okay?

―――

I regretted buying the suitcase well before I dropped it off at Luton airport baggage check. I'd bought an old tan leather case from a second-hand shop, and even with the few things I had packed: T-shirts, swimming trunks and two books, it was heavy.

It had been cheap, in mint condition, and I'd thought it looked more classy than the ones on wheels that everyone else has. I still thought it looked classy, but it seemed likely that I'd arrive on the Costa del Sol with a classy dislocated shoulder.

It was going to be a lonely holiday as Fiona had dumped me, but I'd paid, and wasn't going to let the money go to waste.

―――

I regretted the leather suitcase even more after I put it on my bed in the hotel room, and a man in an old-fashioned black suit and top hat jumped out of it. He ran into the corner of my room, where he remained, staring into the corner and breathing in a way that gave the impression he sucked more air in than he ever breathed out.

"Hey!" I said. But I said it to myself. He wasn't much taller than me, although his top hat was almost tall enough to scrape the room's low, concrete ceiling, but he was easily twice as broad across the shoulders, and his hands were enormous in white satin gloves.

He occupied the corner closest to the balcony doors, where housekeeping had tied up the curtains, making it the darkest part of the room. More gloom seeped out of him with every exhalation.

"Hey!" I said again. This was my room, damn it. I took a step towards him, but made sure to leave the television and its sideboard between us.

His face turned towards me, without the rest of his body moving. It was like a massive moon as it swivelled around over his shoulder to stare in my direction. He had huge black eyes, not round but elongated. They stretched from his temples to within a couple of millimetres of each other over an enormous purple, alcoholic's nose. Underneath the nose, a ragged moustache, almost as wide as his eyes, hung over fat lips. Everything looked like it had been stuck onto the corpse-white, pocked ball of skin that formed his head, like a nightmarish Mr Potato Head.

He took a step towards me, and I grabbed the suitcase and ran, hoping that he was interested in it, rather than me, and I could get rid of him that way.

In the hall, I threw it into one lift, slapping a handful of buttons to make it disappear, before riding the other lift to the lobby.

I told the receptionist that either there was some man in my room, or I was in some man's room. She was able to confirm that the room was mine and sent someone up to make sure he left.

I would have preferred another room, but the hotel was full.

Although I still felt wound up and on edge, I asked the receptionist if she wanted to go for a drink after her shift, because she was blond and petite, and called me "sir," where Fiona had been tall and brunette and called me lots of things (especially in those last few painful weeks), but never "sir."

It was all part of the healing process, as I explained to the doorman, when he turned up to see what all the shouting was about. He suggested I might like to calm down before I returned to my room.

So, I sat in the bar and had some beer. From where I sat, I could see the lifts and every time one opened, I made sure the man with the moon face wasn't inside. After a while, I came up with the idea of asking for towels.

I circled around the lobby, so any of the staff who were watching would think I'd gone up to my room and come back down. Then I lurked behind a group of tourists until a different receptionist was free.

The blonde one had acted just like a Fiona, even if she didn't look like one. I'd gone right off her.

———

A chamber maid eventually appeared with a stack of soft towels as I hung around the corridor near my room. She put them on the bed while I waited outside. The Potato Head figure was still in the corner.

"Anything else, sir?" she asked.

"No." Couldn't she see the man in the corner? Then: "Yes, could you pull the curtains for me?" I asked as she came out.

She hesitated, trying to place me on the hotel's Awkward Guest <—> Sex Fiend Scale.

"I'm afraid of heights," I lied.

She went back in, God bless her, and reached into the corner—surely brushing against the man—and pulled them closed. She kept her eyes fixed on me the whole time, though. As did Potato Head.

When she came back out, it was with a look that dared me to ask for any more favours.

"Thanks," I said, my eyes locked on the figure in the corner. The maid hadn't noticed anything, so he must be there for me.

I went in and closed the door behind me. It was simple: I had gone mad.

The suitcase had been so heavy that I'd burst an important artery in my head from dragging it around. My brain was now drowning in blood, and I was hallucinating all this while dying.

But there's no better comfort for a dying man than plenty of beer—which I'd had—so I decided not to worry too much about it and get some sleep instead.

I woke up a couple of hours later completely disoriented, my throat raw from snoring and bursting for a piss. Somebody was moving in the darkness.

"Fiona?" I croaked.

Then I remembered everything as heavy steps shuffled around the room in the dark. Potato Head's round white face, slit by its ragged gash of moustache, shone as he felt his way to me with outstretched arms.

For all their size, his eyes were obviously useless. They might have been nothing more than decoration. Or camouflage.

I tried to get out of bed, but my legs were tangled in the sheets and I fell head first on the floor. He swivelled at the sound and came straight for me, his hands grabbing and squeezing everything they touched. He found the bed and grasped at the sheets. I quietened my breath as best I could, while lying on my back, with my feet trapped by the bed's tightly made up sheet.

The mattress creaked as he moved along it; the sounds getting slower and softer, as the moon's diffuse glow x-rayed the room through the thin curtains. Its light framed his tall top hat as it crept over the edge of my bed towards me, followed by his huge white face with its sightless eyes. He could hear me, though, and his hands, in their gleaming white satin, reached out for me.

In the morning, I wondered what I'd been so worried about. I'd been scared that the holiday would be lonely without Fiona, but now I enjoyed the companionable silence, as my friend and I stared into our corners of the room. We were waiting for the chambermaid. I hoped it would be the one from yesterday. So small and helpful, she'd suit the third of the room's four corners perfectly.

The rattling of a heavily laden trolley reached us from the corridor. A knock on our door was accompanied by a sing-song "Housekeeping!" and we turned to the sound in unison.

A Love For Now

Ladybirds (that's ladybugs in North America) get their name from Christianity's Virgin Mary, who used to be depicted wearing a red cloak.
It's the same in German, where they're called Marienkäfer *("Mary beetles").*
In Russian, on the other hand, they're "God's little cows."
In this story, I'll be introducing you to a character called the Ladybird Queen.
She has nothing to do with Christianity, nothing to do with virgins, and I wouldn't recommend calling her a cow, either.

The Ladybird Queen lives at the top of the hill. She helps girls like me, if we can find our way to her. There's no path. The base of the hill is a river of tall, thick grass. Trees hide the top.

It's a Sunday morning, everyone else is at Church in their Sunday best. I step off the path into the swirling green river, hoping that my black dress—the one Timothy likes—won't show the grass stains. There's a metallic chittering from all the ladybirds darting around me in the early sunlight and several larger Somethings pushing through the grass around my feet. The grass gets shorter once it realises I won't give up, and I can see the Somethings are birds, glossy crows wambling around my feet, snapping up the ladybirds. There are so many, it doesn't seem to matter, and the birds are too full to fear me.

I know Timothy would never leave his wife. I never asked him to.

"For now," he said. "You're happy with two nights a week for now. You don't mind me being married for now."

But two nights a week is all I want. I like my own company, and even during those first days, when the touch of his fingers on my neck made me catch my breath, when his glance made my skin tingle, I could see he wasn't perfect. Two nights a week really is enough of Timothy, but I must have him for those two nights. The Ladybird Queen can help me.

I push through a tangled hedge and make it to the treeline, leaving thorns bright-tipped with my blood. The shells of ladybirds crunch under my feet. There are no crows here to eat them; the hedge would strip them of their feathers.

My dress is shredded. I may very well end up naked by the time I start my return journey, but it's worth it for two nights with Timothy every week.

On Wednesdays, I like to pretend he's a consultant over from France, but he has to learn English, so he's not allowed to say *Je t'aime*, or anything else. I'm strict with him on Wednesdays.

On Fridays, he visits me instead of taking part in after-work drinks, so that's when I spoil him. I let him drink as much as he wants, and when he falls asleep, I watch over him.

Tenderly, but wondering if this is really all there is to it.

Honestly, twice a week is plenty.

My arms and legs are scratched and scarlet, but I make it to the top of the hill. The Ladybird Queen is beautiful, of course, though it's hard to see her through the swirling clouds of her children flying around. I step towards her and they land on my skin to dip their feet in my blood while I tell the Ladybird Queen what I want.

She tells me I can have my two nights a week and I thank her. As I turn away, I realise I wasted my wish. I should have asked to stay with her here on top of the hill where it's peaceful.

Never mind, two nights with Timothy will be enough. For now, anyway.

When I arrive at the base of the hill again, wondering what it would be like to sleep while the Labybird Queen watched over me, the bodies of all the fat ladybird-fed crows are strewn across the ground. I pick up half a dozen. They're limp and feel smaller than they look. When I shake my fistful of birds, they rattle from all the ladybird shells inside them.

———

Timothy lets me in when I ring his doorbell, but there's panic in his eyes.

It'd be nice to think it's because I'm hurt. My face and arms are so badly scratched that I'm still bleeding. But I think it's because he's never seen me on a Sunday before.

I've baked a pie for him, and his wife is out with the neighbours. I know, because the Ladybird Queen told me, so there's no hurry.

He pulls me into the hallway, which smells of baby sick and talcum powder, before anyone can see me. I tell him it's okay, I know this isn't our time, but that I made him something special.

I warm the crow pie in his wife's kitchen. Once the pastry is golden-brown and steam pipes out of the slit in the centre, I cut him a slice. With the black crows and red ladybird shells it looks festive, like cherry mince pies. He tries it cautiously. It's succulent and tart, and he finishes the whole slice, then goes silent. For now.

———

I wear my silky red dress—the one Timothy always liked—when I dig him up after the funeral. I still prefer my own company to anyone else's, but I feed him a slice of crow pie twice a week: Wednesdays and Fridays. He spends the rest of the time lying in the spare room.

I'll have to go to the Ladybird Queen soon to get more crows, if I want to keep Timothy around.

But there's enough for now.

Not That India

I intended to write a sweetly sad ghost story about what happens when a beloved stuffed toy dies.
Instead, I wrote an odd psychological piece about a comedian trying to take back control of her life.
Please be advised that this story contains some truly dreadful jokes. You have been warned.

———

When Lacey returned from her tour, the tiger was waiting on her bed. She'd left him there on purpose. If she didn't deal with him immediately, then she never would.

So first, she opened the window. The flat always developed a plasticky, refrigerator smell whenever it was unoccupied for more than a few days, and it turned her stomach. She'd managed to overcome her fear of an electrical fire burning the place down to buy a vanilla-scented plug-in air freshener, so now it smelled like a refrigerator with an open yoghurt in it.

A brief August shower mixed the scent of wet concrete with that of London traffic when she opened the kitchen window. The whooshing of cars was all the company she wanted after six weeks on the road, doing stand-up. She was all laughed out.

Back in the hallway, she kicked off her shoes, then ran water on her face. Her skin felt tight from the stage lights, which had picked out every single silvery strand in her dark hair. She took a deep breath, then sat down on the bed beside her tiger, Buzz.

His head flopped to one side and his single eye was grey with washing-machine cataracts. Only a stalk of thread remained from his other eye. She'd never even thought of getting it fixed until now.

He fit perfectly in her cupped hands, but the fabric of his flanks was scratchy, where years of stroking had worn through the weave.

"I'm sorry," she whispered. He didn't reply, obviously. But he knew her thoughts better than she did. It was time to say goodbye. Time for her to grow up before she grew old.

She would have liked to give him to a charity shop, but he was worn out. Nobody else would want him. In the kitchen she unrolled a fresh black plastic bag from under the sink, and wrapped him in it carefully but quickly, before she changed her mind again. It was a Saturday night, and the building was quiet as she made her way to the courtyard to put Buzz in the bin. If she left him in the bin in her own flat, she'd end up getting rising in the middle of the night to take him back. She put him in the recycling bin, rather than with the general waste. It seemed the least she could do. The plastic bag was warm under her hand as she rested it for a moment, then lowered the bin's lid.

"Goodbye," she said, and imagined he mewled a brave *goodbye* back. She took a step away from the bin, then fished him back out. She unwrapped him and set him on the stairs in the hallway. There were lots of families in the building, so he might find a home close by. She gave one of his grubby grey ears a squeeze, then ran back to her apartment.

Cold air had chilled the flat, and the traffic sounded faint. Jeff had told her it was quiet because there were too many electric cars in Dalton. She wasn't sure why he didn't like them, but they were certainly quiet. She closed the window, turned on some music, and tried to write some jokes. If she slept late and ordered in food, she might not have to pass Buzz on the stairs tomorrow, and then he'd be gone.

Without Buzz to revolve around, the flat's gravity felt off. The sitting room yawned too big, and the kitchen was too far away, down a ridiculously long hall, while the bedroom felt cramped from all her clothes. The hairs on her arms and neck tickled.

Nine million people out there, none of whom gave a shit what happened to her.

Her parents had bought Buzz for her before she moved away to University. He had yellow-black stripes and a badge that read "No. 1 Tiger," which she had removed. The needle had gone straight through his chest. When they were alone, together he could fly, if she pushed out her lips to make the *mmeeeeeerrrrrrrr* noise.

She had lost her virginity with Buzz in the bed, his head discreetly turned to one side, as long-haired Mark came while still trying to pull her legs up onto his shoulders. Sam had once tried to wipe himself off on Buzz afterwards. She hadn't thought about them in years, and flipped open her notebook to write.

———

Even after she was making money with her jokes, her parents complained about the waste of her degree, but Lacey had studied philosophy to get out of the house, and thought she was doing pretty well. When she visited them, she brought her notebook rather than Buzz, so she could look forward to coming back to him afterwards.

She brought her notebook everywhere and made notes in it all the time. She filled it with bits of overheard conversation and ideas, but also shopping lists, birthday reminders, and a list of vegetables she should avoid, to see if that was where her increasing stomach cramps came from. On tour, she wrote the addresses of her gigs and hotels in advance, so that she didn't have to rely on her phone's battery.

It was also full of scribbles, circles, and stars, and page after page of doodled birds and flying tigers. When she visited her parents, her mother sat on the edge of the couch, as if in readiness for all Lacey's news, should she have any this time, while her father pretended to watch the television. Lacey could never think of anything to tell them and the notebook allowed her to say, "Excuse me, idea!" and disappear into it.

Lacey didn't have any memories of her mother outside the house, and only one of her father: at the beach, his fists planted on his hips, one on each side of his beer belly, as he inspected the sea. When he was satisfied with it, he turned and stretched out his arms for Lacey to run into, before letting her go.

It was from when she was a lot younger, of course.

Lacey had met Jeff at an open-mic night. She told jokes, and he did impressions.

He didn't mind sharing the bed with Buzz. In fact, he did a good impression of him.

His favourite joke of hers was, "When people say 'love hurts,' they're talking about anal."

But something had gone wrong.

Or perhaps not, and they had always just been best friends, sleeping with each other by mistake.

Jeff rang the next morning.

"Hey Lace, did you knock 'em dead?"

"What time is it?"

"Yeah. Me and Becky are going kayaking. You want to meet up for coffee afterwards?"

No. "Who's Becky?"

"Funny. See you at the Bazaar."

After she hung up, she remembered Buzz was on the stairs.

But there was no sign of him when she left the flat. The step was empty, and she sat on it for a moment to wish him well. But quietly, in her head, so that he wouldn't hear it. She should give him a chance to get used to life with someone else.

Lacey walked to Primrose Hill to see Jeff and Becky off. She had never gone kayaking, but it was better than being in the flat where the Buzz-shaped hole rang like tinnitus. They were tugging on neoprene wetsuits when she arrived. She liked Becky. She liked all of Jeff's girlfriends, and it wasn't even awkward with him standing there smiling at them both, before moving off to shout good-naturedly at someone already in the water. When he turned back, his paunch pushed against the wetsuit, giving Becky a comfortable cushion to land on, when she ran to him to get her wetsuit zipped up.

When they were in their kayaks, Lacey noticed Becky's broad shoulders. They suited her. Lacey liked broad shoulders on a woman; it looked strong.

She was glad she didn't have them herself, though, they wouldn't have suited her. Their smooth, tight-fitting wetsuits made Becky and Jeff look like shaved gorillas.

Or plastic monkeys.

Monkey-shaped balloons.

She wrote that down in her notebook, then walked back to Dalston to wait for them at the Bazaar, near Ridley Road. She had her notebook, so it was work.

Jeff insisted on buying coffees to warm up when he arrived with Becky. The girl behind the counter laughed at something he said, while she added three tiny water glasses to his tray. She was young, with long black hair pulled into a tight ponytail. Becky stared at Lacey, then asked her for her autograph, which made both of them blush.

"Good tour?" asked Jeff, as they waited for their turn with the single spoon he had brought to share out the sugar. It was his way of asking if she'd hooked up with anyone. Becky leaned her head on his arm, her long dark hair still damp.

Lacey shrugged noncommittally. Nobody worth mentioning. Nobody she'd have introduced to Buzz.

The flat stank when she got back. Coffee grounds, carrots and pan grease. It was worse than the refrigerator smell. It smelled like the bins, but she'd emptied them before she'd gone on tour, and she'd seen they were still empty last night. She checked the toilet hadn't backed up as the smell intensified, then opened a window.

She made a cup of tea and tried to turn her monkey-shaped balloons into a joke. Her career was gaining momentum. She needed to keep working, get material for a new show as quickly as possible. A cat mewled outside, lonely in the big city, and she decided to take a break.

For dinner, she cooked fish fingers and mashed potatoes. It was a combination of comfort food and punishment. The fish fingers' box had been in her freezer for so long that it was encrusted in ice. The mashed potato was freeze-dried yellow flakes from a stiff plastic sachet.

Lacey loved fish fingers when her mother made them, but she couldn't cook them herself. If she cooked them until the breadcrumbs were golden brown, like the box said, then the white fish centre remained cold. She had to cook them until she had burned the exterior black. She added them to the plate of mashed potatoes and ate in front of the television, worrying that she was giving herself cancer.

Lacey suffered from sleep paralysis. Sometimes she could wake from it, but it required effort. She needed to force out a dry-throated groan to break the spell, and be able to move again. It used to terrify Jeff.

The internet said it was the time lag between when the brain and the body woke up, but it always felt like a hell of a long time before her body came back under her own control. She had a recurring nightmare about someone breaking in while she was asleep and attacking her while she was paralysed.

Her breath shuddered as something moved on the bed, a tiny shifting weight, like a rat. Her lungs ached with the need to suck in air to groan, to wake herself up, to scare it away, but they were frozen.

She told herself it must be a cat. A rat would go straight for her eyes. The bin-stink of carrots, coffee grounds and pan grease seeped into her lungs and the shape mewled. Her arms lay dead at her sides and her throat strained to force out the groan that would let her move.

The shape mewled again. *Buzz!* She had missed him so much after only one day. He padded around on her bed, as tears welled and rolled down the sides of her face, until he found the best place to sleep. *Buzz!*

She called in her mind, but he didn't answer. Which was odd, because, after all, she did the talking for both of them. She was old enough to know that.

The next time she looked at her phone, it told her it was morning. The bed was empty beside her, though her room stank of the bins, so she put on old clothes, a scarf over her hair, and oversized tinted glasses, which she thought looked retro-cool, to search for him. Perhaps Buzz hadn't found a new home, after all.

Mrs Clarke from upstairs took it upon herself to keep the stairs and hallways free of flyers, and to make sure that no one left shoes or anything else out in case of fire. There was no sign of Buzz's yellow-black fur in the paper bin, so she checked the others, lifting and sorting between the bags, in case someone had moved him, or trapped him by adding another one on top. She couldn't find him, so perhaps he had climbed into a bag. They were warm and sticky, and puffed out sweet rot when she ripped them open, combing her fingers through old food and paper towels. A clump of hair exploded out of one, nappies from another. No Buzz.

Lacey sat on the stairs to work it out. If Buzz was in the bin, then he couldn't have visited her last night. And if he had visited her, then he wouldn't have gone back in the bin. So, where was he? Brown slime had engrained itself into her hands and lodged itself under her fingernails. She sniffed it and decided it might once have been a banana.

Jeff texted, which was the perfect distraction. She had a set planned for the end of the week, but only had a couple of new jokes, and didn't think either of them worked unless she explained them, and jokes weren't funny if you explained them. Unless you were Stewart Lee, of course, because then the explanation *was* the joke. Jeff might know how to get them to work.

He was uncharacteristically quiet when he arrived. Like he had used to be, back when they were best friends who slept with one another and had fought. After a few hours, and a few drinks, he asked if he could stay the night.

"Of course."

"You should try to meet someone," he said. "I can't have you still pining for me."

"I met someone on tour," she said. "But he wasn't interested."

Jeff stretched out on the couch as she got up. "Yeah?"

"Yeah. He was into this other girl. She was hot. From Mumbai. Really hot, you know? Young, skinny, long dark hair."

"Yeah?"

"She wasn't interested in him. Maybe 'cause she was Hindu? I don't know. The whole situation was ridiculous."

"Maybe he was too keen," said Jeff.

"He asked me what I thought. To see if I could suggest anything to, like, curry favour with her."

"Yeah?"

"I told him straight, I said, 'Look: she's just not that India.'"

Jeff snorted, and then his phone vibrated.

When the sitting room had gone quiet, she sneaked through her own apartment to the front door. The building breathed around her, but there was a hole in it where her tiger should have been.

Buzz? She thought his name as hard as she could and directed it down the steps. Just in case. After a moment, she closed the door again and went back to bed, propping herself on her pillows to make sure she stayed awake so she wouldn't miss him if he came back.

A weight woke her when it pushed down on the mattress, rolling her to one side. It was bigger than Buzz.

Jeff.

And only her mind was awake as he slipped under the covers. She tried to groan, but it wouldn't come. She heard another sound from behind Jeff, and thought, *Becky's here, and she's going to shoot us both, or at least cut Jeff's dick off,* followed by *Good!*

She heard the sound again, but didn't recognise it, because Buzz had never growled before. He pounced onto the bed and bit Jeff's head off with a single bite.

Jeff fell back, blood squirting from his neck. And it must be a different tiger. How could Buzz have grown so quickly and

Jeff fell back. Warm blood squirted on her face, and it was Buzz! He reared up, huge, and growled in her head, *RRRRRRR!* and

Jeff fell back, his arms splayed like he wanted to prop them on his hips. And Buzz had learned how to take care of himself and

Jeff fell back. And she couldn't move, and Buzz was huge and angry and

Jeff fell back into Buzz's mouth. Buzz clacked his teeth and his throat swelled as he swallowed Jeff whole.

———

The sun was up when Lacey could move again. After the sleep paralysis, the weight of Buzz had kept her pinned to the mattress. She pretended to sleep until he purred.

In the morning, Buzz had shrunk back to his proper size when she finally opened her eyes. Her skin felt tight, like something had dried on it overnight. Buzz purred when she picked him up to hold him close.

"I looked for you," she said.

He fixed her with his single good eye. When she got up, she dug out a tiny sewing kit that she had stolen from a hotel. But he was proud of his missing eye. He was a real tiger now and liked his scars. She changed the sheets and threw the old ones away. They stank of coffee grounds and pan grease and carrots.

"Where were you?" she asked when they crawled into the fresh blankets. She spoke out loud because she wanted to know for real, not make it up in her head.

He ignored her, so she apologised.

"Sorry," she said. *Sorry, sorry, sorry.* She cried and Buzz let her kiss him until they were friends again.

Best friends? she thought, and Buzz growled. Because she was best friends with Buzz, and best friends with Jeff, and look at what had happened there.

She squeezed him, and he relented. Best friends, he agreed. It almost sounded like the old Buzz. Lacey and Buzz. Best friends.

———

"I caught a mate of mine playing with his monkey." She was onstage and paused for a couple of chuckles. "Well… he had a straw up its bum, inflating the poor thing. With a hairdryer. The monkey didn't look happy, I can tell you. Just big. And he kept getting bigger. And hotter. My mate had taped the hairdryer's nozzle around one end of the straw, so all the hot air was rushing up the monkey's bum and he just kept expanding! I mean, I don't like to interfere and my mate, Patrick, had the car running outside, so he was ready to go to the vet if something went wrong, but it seemed odd, I had to ask. We were all out in the garden by this stage, because the monkey was too big to fit indoors anymore. And when I asked him what he was doing, he said, 'I've always wanted to go for a ride with a hot-air *baboon*.'"

A few chuckles again, but she'd lost them.

Move on.

She had two stools for her act. She sat on one, Buzz on the other. "Well, let me introduce you to my assistant," she said, waving her arm to indicate him.

No one laughed, and she realised where she had gone wrong. If he had still been a cute little tiger, it might have been funny, but he was a full-sized predator and it set the wrong tone.

That was his cue, however, so he opened his mouth, and she put her head inside, wearing an expression of terror, which earned her a few laughs.

She had a funny face.

The joke, of course, was that she wasn't pretending.

The Drowned Man's Upside-Down Grin

I wanted to try my hand at urban legends. This is it.
Watch out for the Drowned Man.
Watch out for the Night Sea.
Pass it on.

The Drowned Man is under our bed, which rocks as he scuffles over the floor.

Under the floor.

Outside, the convenience store's flashing red "OPEN" sign paints the dark bedroom alternately blood red and tar black through the thin curtains. The flickering pulls the walls and towers of unpacked cardboard boxes closer, then further away, like the bed is adrift at sea.

I should never have done it.

His scrabbling as he crawled under the gap in the door towards the bed I share with my brother Ben is what woke me, and my thin night dress is no protection against the chills running down my spine as I wait for his shark-like face—wide as a shovel, pale as a corpse, the upside-down grin full of jagged thumb-sized teeth—to rise out of the night sea below the floorboards.

A pale shadow crawls on hands and knees from the bed to the cardboard boxes, rippling the floorboards over its back as it moves, like the floor is nothing more than water. The tower trembles as his snout sniffs at them from under the floor.

My brother is still asleep beside me. "Ben!" I whisper, and the bed jolts as the shark-faced Drowned Man darts back towards us, his arms and legs moving lizard-like, in case we try to leave.

I didn't want Ben to die, I just wanted to scare him enough to stop him from pissing the bed. At school the other girls make fun of him—and me—because of it, but the video didn't say what to do when you change your mind. I don't want the Drowned Man to drag either of us into the frigid night sea, where he hunts.

Outside, a car takes the corner of Hope and Somerset too close, the wheels making a sticky ripping noise as the rubber grinds the curb. Further away, a siren howls at the moon. Inside, there's Ben's almost-snore from his blocked, snotty nose, and the scratching of the monster under the bed.

I lie right in the faded piss stain in the middle of the old mattress to keep away from the edges, where the huge grin—a black rip in the white blubber of his face—could appear at any moment.

I want Ben to wake up, but what if he screams? Sharks echo-locate, don't they? In the crimson flashing darkness, my mind replays the last scene of the YouTube video over and over again, and I see the Drowned Man's hungry smile everywhere around us.

The new flat only has one bedroom, and Ma is sleeping on the couch. She coughs, and I shut my eyes. I don't want him to eat my Ma, but the thin mattress moves under me to let me know he's staying here. It's Ben he wants. Or me, if he can't have him.

———

Take a bath by the light of a single candle.

Afterwards, splash 13 drops of your blood down the centre of the whirlpool of escaping water onto the drain's metal grille.

Blow out the candle, and the Drowned Man will cross the night sea to find you.

———

I didn't use my blood. I used Ben's.

Just to scare him. So he'd stop wetting the bed we have to share until Ma gets better, gets back on her feet, and I get my own one again.

I made him watch the video of the thickset man in Cambodia, an ex-Marine, whose trick was sitting unprotected in a saltwater pool while a Great White shark sucked up chunks of bloody chum around him.

All the way to the end, where the Great White grabbed the man's leg, holding him under till he drowned.

The very end, where the dead man's face just breaks the surface, and the light reflects off the water so that it looks like he has a white shovel-shaped shark's face now, too.

I read Ben the comment about summoning the Drowned Man, showed him the blood I'd saved from that time he'd cut his lip on the glass I'd told him not to drink from.

Told him if he ever pissed the bed again, then the Drowned Man would make him stop.

It worked.

Ben's sleeping peacefully and hasn't wet the bed since.

So how do I get rid of the monster?

My mother starts coughing in the other room.

"Beth!" When she gets enough breath back she calls me and the floorboards bulge and ripple towards the other room, as the Drowned Man goes looking to see who else wants me.

"Beth!" Her voice is choked, like she's suffocating between the goopy barking coughs. It's just the flu. She'll be fine. The Drowned Man doesn't want her.

She keeps coughing, and I tell myself it's a trick, the Drowned Man trying to lure me out of bed. It's not my mother at all who groans out an exhausted "Please!"

I tell myself I'm asleep and dreaming. Or I'm losing my mind from the ammonia fumes of Ben's piss, which used to wake me most nights.

I tell myself that it won't be my fault if she gets up for water and the Drowned Man grabs her.

I make a promise to look after Ben for the rest of my life, if that happens though, because I know it's a lie.

Her feet thump the floorboards, and my stomach clenches. My head pounds as I wait for the splash and snap of the Drowned Man's mouth, pulling her into the night sea with his awful teeth.

I'm sorry, Ma, I think, too short of breath to say the goodbye out loud.

But her feet keep slapping the floorboards.

I jump and let out a scream when the kitchen light clicks on. The faucet runs, then her feet slap towards me.

"You didn't hear me?" She's in the doorway, face waxy and tired. I rub my eyes, pretending to wake, but scanning the shadows behind her. They jump in the light of the mute TV she leaves on for company, but there's no bony dead man, no shark face creeping up on her.

"Ma?"

"You aren't getting sick, too, are you?" The coughing has ripped her throat, her voice is hoarse. I tell her I'm fine. She nods and turns to go, has to hold the wall for a minute to cough up her other lung.

"Go back to bed," I say. I shouldn't have let her get up, but it's easy to be brave with her there and the light on. "I'll call work. Let them know you're not coming in tomorrow." The night shift will take the message.

The shock of the cold on my bare feet—the relief of the solid floor—makes me gasp, and I bunch my toes, revelling in the chill, the grit of our unswept floor. I bring her back to bed.

Ben sleeps through the whole thing.

"There's something goin' around," they say when I call, so I tuck Ma in tightly.

The flat is still too dark, but it's a relief to be out of the bedroom, and the TV's blue light is better than the bedroom's sly red, so I sit with her, my legs curled up under me, under my nightdress. I'm too exhausted to sleep.

Eventually I doze, jerking awake every time the TV screen darkens, dreaming the Drowned Man is blocking the light. Dozing is when you have the worst nightmares, and my legs are numb from the cold, as there isn't another blanket other than the one

Ma has. The next time I wake up, my legs are sprawled out on the floor, so it looks like there isn't a monster waiting to drag me away after all, and I can't afford to get sick, too. Looks like whoever left that YouTube comment was full of shit.

Who'd have thought, huh?

I go to bed, determined not to look at the jumping shadows around me which have raised the hairs on my neck, my arms.

It occurs to me that, even if the guy drowned, why would he have a shark's face?

One comment said that he was born like that. It was because he looked so much like a shark that he could safely do his trick. Except that's bullshit, too, because the shark killed him. It was just the light reflecting off the water in the grainy footage that gave him the white face, the shadows of ripples that gave him the enormous down-turned shark's mouth, the staring holes for eyes.

The stale tang of the air in the bedroom is enough to burn my nose, but at least I don't smell pee. Maybe I am getting sick and was sweating out a fever dream. I crawl into my side of the bed and imagine how good it's going to be when we have separate beds again. Ben is on the far side, wrapped up in his *Ben 10* covers. Maybe he's sick too. We can all go to the doctor together, Ma, and me, and Ben. He's not a bad kid. Could he have cystitis? That makes people pee.

The bed is so wet that I wonder if he has pissed in it again after all, and that's all I need, but it doesn't stink. I roll myself into my own bedspread and, wouldn't you know it? *That* wakes him up. He rolls towards me into the middle of the bed.

"Forget it," I say. We have a rule. "Bed-wetters sleep on the edge."

The words stick in my throat. It's not Ben. The bed is covered in blood, the sticky patch blending into black waves which roll and break in the shadows underneath the unfurling bed cover: the night sea.

Phosphorescent seaweed beckons me, and the Drowned Man grins at me from where my little brother should be. His shark's smile is upside-down as if he regrets what he's about to do.

The black holes of his eyes tell a different story, though. He wraps his thin freezing arms—too thin for that massive head—around me, pressing the bones of his elbows and knees into me, dragging me with him, as he slides down the shores of the sheets into the dark under the covers, where the water is deepest.

Saltwater rushes into my throat before I can scream. His sad smile opens to swallow me whole.

The Heavy Air Above the Clouds

An article about someone who wanted to bring their support peacock onboard a plane inspired this fantasy mystery about a talking ostrich who hates flying.
I wrote the first draft while we were on holidays, but kept it top-secret until we had safely flown back home to Kazakhstan. My wife hates flying, too…

Two policemen bundled the ostrich into the interrogation room, where she was waiting to assess his mental condition. The ostrich, which the police file identified only as "Reinhold", gave her a single confused glance as he lowered himself gingerly onto the tiny metal chair bolted to the floor opposite her. The chair was the right size for humans, but far too small for an ostrich to sit comfortably, and far too close to be safe if he became dangerous. His long pale neck poked out of his ill-fitting orange jumpsuit, adding to the impression of absent-minded harmlessness.

"You want handcuffs? He's big," asked one of the two police officers who'd delivered him to her.

What good were handcuffs, when he could whip his neck over the table and snap her arm or peck out an eye with his beak? He might look confused, but he'd already killed one woman.

And he's not human, she reminded herself. Ostriches always look confused. Don't anthropomorphize.

She ignored the question and addressed the ostrich, waiting for the men to leave. "My name is Dr Lorenz, and the police are interested in what happened to Miss Roberts. But I'm here for you, Reinhold. As soon as the officers leave, we can talk about whatever you'd like."

Then she waited for them to go, while Reinhold stared at the diamond-shaped shadow his head cast on the table. Every time she turned up at the station, she had to put up with the same thing, the officers openly patronising about her profession, or condescendingly offering the "little lady" their help. After a long minute of them hanging around to make sure she got a good whiff of their offended testosterone, they left.

"Cold," said one as he banged the door closed.

Reinhold still hadn't shown any reaction, so she let the silence of the room unfold until the swishing of footsteps along the corridor and muffled sound of talking coming through the heavy door became claustrophobic in the small room. Even with human occupants, the room would be cramped. Sitting across from a nine-foot tall, 150 pound ostrich made it oppressive.

Reinhold's claws scratched softly but restlessly at the floor, a sign of agitation which drew the psychologist's attention to his long, thick legs. His jumpsuit only reached to just above his knees. Either they hadn't been able to find something that fit or, more likely, they hadn't cared enough to bother.

Although he still didn't move, she noticed the atmosphere changed as soon as she flipped open the case notes folder. She had always been sensitive to atmosphere.

"The police are still searching for Miss Roberts, Reinhold. Can you tell me anything about that? You were the last one to see her alive."

As she had expected, Reinhold ignored the question and its implications.

"Well, this isn't the first time you've been in trouble." She pretended to read it from the case file. "How about we start with that?"

"I didn't do anything." His voice was petulant, and he jabbed his beak at the manilla folder. With the fluttering of fine feathers on his head, it gave him the mien of a grumpy, absent-minded professor. "I don't care what it says in there."

"Okay," said Dr Lorenz. "One thing it doesn't tell me in here is how you got the name 'Reinhold.' Care to tell me about that?"

"Because I'm so sweet," said Reinhold. "That's what Emma said." Dr Lorenz wasn't sure how to parse Reinhold's reaction. She'd have expected a human accused of murder to accompany the statement with an ironic twist of the lips, but, of course, Reinhold's beak was incapable of that kind of movement, and his tone was even.

"She used to work with a guy who ate sugar cubes as a snack. His name was Reinhold," he explained, as if he thought that was what she was most interested in. But it had got him talking.

"'Emma' is Miss Roberts, right?"

"Ten years I helped her, I can call her Emma. She told me to."

"Where is Emma now?"

"How would I know?"

"She was your owner."

Reinhold's neck jerked back to drink in the therapist with his large chestnut-coloured eyes. Dr Lorenz tried to hold his gaze, but his eyes were unfocussed. He was deep in his own thoughts, his own head.

"She was my *friend*," he said.

"She might be in trouble. Your friend might need help."

"She's gone," said Reinhold. His voice was faint. "Ten years I was her support. I took her to the mall, to the cinema, to the sea. She was scared of everything." He trailed off.

"She 'was' scared of everything?"

That got his attention. Beak or not, his mouth curled sarcastically. "Yeah, she 'was' scared of everything. And then she 'wasn't.' I helped her conquer the fear."

"Even flying?"

"She shouldn't have made me. I told her!" He shouted the last agitated words, then ducked and weaved his head, as if to hide. But there was nowhere in the bare room for an ostrich to bury his head. Dr Lorenz waited for him to calm down, consciously relaxing her own breathing and ignoring the sweat that had prickled in her armpits, the flash of cold down her spine. She had a thin aerosol can of Mace tucked between her thigh and her chair. If he got physical, she'd have to move faster than he did, that was all.

"Let's talk about the first time the police arrested you, Reinhold," she said.

"I didn't do anything."

"You caused Flight J620 to make an emergency landing in Dulles airport, injuring two flight attendants and causing the current ban on support animals on planes."

"We shouldn't have been up there. I hate flying."

Was that where the frustration came from? The bird being forced to sit in the plane, reminded of what it could never do itself?

"Did you resent Emma for making you fly?"

"We had an agreement." Reinhold was looking around the room, his claws scraping over the floor as he got worked up.

Dr Lorenz found it hard to breathe, as if the air was getting denser around them. Pushing him much further would be a mistake, but they were close to a breakthrough. She could taste it. The hair on her neck stood up, with the sense of anticipation in the room. Was she picking up the officers' excitement behind their two-way mirror?

"Where is Emma's body?" There was no point pretending the woman was still alive. She'd already been missing for over two months.

"She wanted to fly, so I taught her to fly. I told her They wouldn't like it," said Reinhold. "It wasn't my fault!"

No matter what she tried after that, he wouldn't say anything else, but the atmosphere in the cell-like room remained electric, so that it was a surprise to find the room behind the two-way mirror empty when she entered. While Reinhold had been talking, she had had the impression of being the focus of attention.

He must have been thinking things over, because after the officers dumped him in his seat at the next meeting, Reinhold wouldn't shut up. Or perhaps it was the pressure of the cells, which weren't built to hold him. Or the other prisoners, who surely made their resentment of his celebrity status clear.

It suited her fine though, because the pressure was mounting on her, too. There was still no sign of Miss Roberts' body. In fact, there was no sign of a crime at all, other than the original bloodstain and the fact that she was missing. The manhunt already extended across state lines, and the FBI would swoop in sooner rather than later. Reinhold had been an unwilling public figure ever since the events on Flight J620. It would reflect badly on them if they didn't close the case.

The same two police officers brought him, and they didn't bother asking about handcuffs. She was sure they half-hoped Reinhold would attack her, teach her a lesson. They said nothing at all, and she ignored them right back. Their opinion of her didn't matter. She wasn't here to make friends. She was here to help solve a case. Give her career a boost, too, if she was lucky.

Reinhold talked easily when she asked him. Dr Lorenz assumed he was getting the silent treatment in the holding cells and pitied him for what was coming next. As lonely as prison could get, the silence was usually the precursor to violence.

"Support's a good gig. It depends on the client, but I liked Emma right from the start. There's the prestige, too. You're not like a pet dog; I studied at college to help people. And there's lots of hugging. I like hugs." Reinhold was telling it all to the corner of the room, his voice dreamy, rather than faint. Lost in happier days. Nonetheless, the air in the room felt electric, like a storm was about to break. Dr Lorenz tasted the weight of the charged atmosphere between her teeth.

"Hugs are nice," she agreed.

"I just didn't want to fly. I was so happy when the airlines stopped it. But Emma was angry. With me!"

"The airlines stopped allowing support animals because of you, Reinhold."

"We had to get off that plane!"

"You were 30,000 feet up."

"We should never have gone up. We had to get off!"

"You attacked the flight attendants."

"I was defending myself. They panicked when I told them what was happening. *Everyone* was panicking. That's how close we were."

"They had fractured ribs. Miss Hoyle had a compound fracture in her right arm. Mr Cummings almost lost an eye. He spent seven hours on the operating table."

"I didn't mean for anyone to get hurt. I just needed to get us down. Thanks to me, we landed safe and sound."

"The flight attendants were badly injured."

Reinhold's voice hardened. "They might have ended up a damn sight worse."

"And why there? Why Dulles?"

"Blame the captain for that. I just wanted to get back on the ground. Even if it was Dulles."

"You said they panicked when you told them what was happening. What exactly did you tell them?" Dr Lorenz leaned over the table, even as her training told her not to crowd the patient like that. It was like someone else was controlling her, using her to find out what Reinhold knew. But just like after his arrest—for attempted hijacking and aggravated assault—Reinhold clammed up, as if he'd said too much. Was there someone else involved that he was trying to protect, or was this part of his delusion?

"Was Emma happy that you'd got down safe and sound?" she said.

"I guess she never believed me, and she was hooked on flying, despite how it turned out. Blamed me for what happened. But we agreed on one time. One time. She knew They didn't like it."

"So, what happened then?" asked Dr Lorenz after a few minutes, avoiding any questions about *Them*, in case it shut him up again.

"Well, there were no more hugs." Reinhold barked a laugh. "She put me in the *garden*. After all, we'd been through!"

"And then?"

He stared at his feet. "I showed her how to fly," he muttered, then paused. "I guess I really showed her, didn't I?"

"Did you, Reinhold? Nobody knows, because nobody can find her. Your friend is missing."

"Yeah, well. I showed her how to fly, and she flew away."

"The cops say you threw her out the window. Is that how you made her fly?"

"We used to go swimming together. She was afraid of the water, said it was too murky to see if there was something coming for her."

"*Did* you throw her out the window, Reinhold? Is that where the blood came from?"

"Hated the mall. Too many people. Too much noise, not enough space. No way to hear if trouble showed up. Nowhere to hide if it did. But together we used to go."

"Tell me where Emma is, Reinhold."

"Scared of the circus, scared of cats, scared of snakes, scared of heights. Scared of what was in her pills. Scared she'd *forget* her pills. Scared of blue plastic. Can you believe that? Couldn't bear to have blue plastic anywhere in the house when I met her. Said there were faces in it. I helped her through it all. You don't know how damn good I was. But flying was always the big one. She always wanted to fly. So, finally, when the airlines wouldn't let us on again, I showed her how to do it. God help me!"

"Why show her? If it's so dangerous?"

"Because it's what she wanted! Haven't you ever been in love? You want them to be happy, so you give them what they want. You're afraid they'll stop loving you, if you don't." Reinhold started crying. "People fly every day and nothing happens. There are men in suits who spend half their lives flying back and forth from one meeting to another, and nothing happens. I thought we'd be okay, we were just going to go up *once*! She promised. But They were waiting for us. They knew I knew They were there."

It was the first time Reinhold had revealed stronger feelings for his owner than just friendship, but Dr Lorenz had suspected as much. "Who was waiting for you, Reinhold? Where's Emma?"

"As soon as I showed her how to fly, I started waking up in an empty house. I guessed what she was doing, but she always said she was shopping. And she was happy, so if she was doing it in the woods, like I showed her, I thought she'd be okay. One morning she didn't come back. They'd taken her."

"Who took her?"

"What's with you people? You know They're up there: the gods. God. Whatever They are. All that space, and you think there's *nothing* up there?"

A chill ran down her back, and she had to swallow before continuing. "There's no one up there, Reinhold. You were the last one to see her alive."

"You're not scared of flying, are you?" Now that they were finally talking about it, he had relaxed. She couldn't have said the same for herself, though. Jitters, like she'd overdosed on coffee, made her want to get up and walk around. Made her want to get out of there. Made her nervous, like he was going to tell her something she'd regret forever.

"No," she said.

"Then I guess you're not as sensitive as you like to think. I thought you felt it. I don't usually make mistakes about that."

The barb was unexpected and hit a sore spot. She prided herself on being able to pick up on things. And she had been picking up a weird sense of density in the room whenever Reinhold started talking.

"Even if there was someone up there, how would you know about it? People can't fly, nor can ostriches." She almost hoped he'd clam up again. She'd prefer it, if it meant she didn't have to listen to any more of his crap.

"Ha!"

"What does that mean?"

"It means: 'can't' or 'won't?' Sensitive people understand. That's why they get scared. They feel Them. Here." He raised a wing to point awkwardly to the back of his long neck. "When They see you, it's like you can't breathe right. Like an itch. That's what had everyone on J620 panicking. Even the goddamn frequent flyers felt it, that's how close we got to Them. They were looking right at us, and when They look at you, you get out of the air!"

The door slammed open and the same two officers walked in. "Time's up, bird." They dragged him to his feet.

"Wait!" said Dr Lorenz.

"Time's up," said one, while the other grinned at her.

"What about the blood, Reinhold? The police found her blood under the trees," she said.

"Then that's where They grabbed her." The police pushed Reinhold through the door.

"Come on, Reinhold, people can't fly." She followed them out into the hallway, but Reinhold let his head droop as he was dragged back to his cell.

———

She dreaded the interviews with Reinhold. Despite his previous insult, Dr Lorenz knew she was sensitive, and the atmosphere was oppressive when they talked. He was either dangerously psychotic or dangerously manipulative. Or maybe they were just a bad fit. Sometimes that happened, too, and he was suffering as much as she was. But this would be the last interview. The prosecutor was pushing them to trial, even though everything they had was circumstantial. She didn't doubt they'd get a conviction, anyway.

Reinhold would be appointed an overworked public defender, and all the prosecution had to do was get him on the stand talking about how They were waiting, and how he had taught Miss Roberts to fly.

A bruise darkened his eye when he entered the room, and several nasty cuts disfigured his neck. He was missing feathers, too, but he walked tall between the police officers, and she saw how they were suddenly wary around him. She'd assumed being so different would make prison life hard for him, but it looked like he'd worked out how to make the best of it. Being so big could be an advantage behind bars.

"I didn't expect you back again," he said.

So he already knew. "I'm sorry, there's nothing I can do for you, Reinhold."

"No sweat."

"You're going to prison, Reinhold. There's no way a jury will accept that Miss Roberts flew away. But we have an hour to talk about anything you want."

After a pause, Reinhold spoke. "They call me 'Professor.' I like that." He smiled at her, leaning back in his seat, forcing her to look up to meet his gaze. He didn't say anything else, but his silence was relaxed. Whatever had been on his mind was no longer an issue.

Eventually, she broached the topic that had been bothering her. "You do understand that ostriches can't fly, don't you, Reinhold? Off the record?" If she prevented him from making a fool of himself in prison—something which could end in a fatality—by claiming he could fly, then she'd have achieved something.

"Birds can fly. Ostriches are birds. Ergo, ostriches can fly."

He was settling into his role as the Professor, but she wouldn't let it stand. "Ostriches can't fly."

"Ostriches *won't* fly. See, small birds like crows and seagulls, and... whatever are okay. They're small, they don't get noticed. *They* ignore them. Or They don't even see them. But an ostrich, or a goddamn airplane. That's big enough for Them to notice."

"And They don't like it?" There was nothing she could do while he held onto his absurd delusion, but if this was what he wanted to talk about, then fine. Already, though, the familiar sense of pressure, of being watched, started to build.

"I guess not. They don't even like being talked about. Perhaps *They* think They're gods, and don't want anyone else up there. Or maybe just anything in the sky is fair game."

"How come you didn't mention any of this before?"

He rolled his eyes. "Because you'd have completely believed me, right?"

"I understand that you've created an unhealthy coping mechanism to deal with the fact that you can't fly."

"Can. Won't. Not ever again." He didn't care what she said. Even going to prison didn't bother him. She tried one last time, anyway. "If you tell me where Miss Roberts' body is, then your attorney could try to cut a deal."

"I don't know where she is. I told you, she flew, so They took her."

"People can't fly any more than ostriches can, Reinhold."

"Exactly. People can do anything once they know how."

"Then show m—"

"No! Listen, there won't be any red eye flights for me in prison, so I appreciate your help, but I'm going to be fine. And you've probably got enough material for your next book, or whatever it is, so let's just agree to disagree, okay?"

"How did you know I'm writing a book?"

"You're a psychologist. Of course you're writing a book." He winked at her.

She exhaled a deep breath, releasing the tension from all the previous interviews. "I'll be talking about you at an upcoming conference, actually. Even though I feel like I failed."

"You did fine," he said. "Where's the conference? The Hyatt downtown?"

"Boston."

He stared at her. "How are you getting there?"

"Flying," she said, and her stomach dropped as he jumped out of his seat.

"What?" He towered over her. "Are you crazy? You haven't listened to a damn thing I've said! Stay off the planes. Stay off them, you hear?" He jabbed his head towards her, probably just to shout in her face, but she already had the Mace in her hand and blasted him in the eyes.

He stumbled back, coughing and retching. The door burst open as officers stormed in. "Stay off the planes!" yelled Reinhold as best he could, with a throat full of Mace. "They'll be waiting for you! Stay off the damn planes!"

He kept trying to get to her, as she trembled in shock. More officers ran in, jumping into the melee until they had him restrained. The last thing she heard, as they manhandled him down the corridor, was: "Stay on the ground. Planes don't crash, they get *thrown!*"

She had almost decided against the conference. The thought of Reinhold—her failure—had left a nasty taste in her mouth, but while talking to a colleague to decompress, she'd mentioned what he'd said about Miss Roberts seeing faces in blue plastic. Seeing faces, pareidolia, was nothing new, but the specificity of seeing them only in blue plastic had led them into a whole new arena for research, and she was eager to present their first findings, to mark the territory as their own.

As she sat in the taxi on the way to the airport, she was so engrossed in her notes that she barely noticed the gathering storm clouds. As always, the streets had snarled up all the traffic around the airport. Eventually, she noticed they weren't moving and looked up to see what was happening.

Through the window, she noticed the low, heavy clouds. It would be a bumpy flight, if it wasn't cancelled. She stared at them a while longer. They hung unusually low, giving the impression that she could almost reach them if she were to stand on the cab's roof. They writhed over the highway. Over her taxi.

One of the unfortunate side-effects of researching pareidolia was that she saw faces everywhere, too. She sought them out to understand her subjects better. She could see one right now, hanging in the middle of the clouds and staring straight back at her, through the taxi's window. It was enormous, two city blocks wide, but not human. Two extra dark patches of cloud were sunken eye sockets, and the twisting of the cloud gave it a mass of writhing tentacles for a nose, reaching down towards her. She could swear they were sniffing the air around her taxi, while the mouth was a cruel eagle's beak.

It made her think of Reinhold for the first time in weeks. Had he seen something like this? Was this what had pushed him over the edge into delusion? It was all too easy to believe. The hairs on the back of her neck were not merely standing up, they were vibrating, and she found it difficult to breathe in, as if the air had got heavy. Her lungs itched the way they did when she went skiing and took her first gulp of sub-zero air. Even worse, though, was the feeling of being observed.

Even as the clouds bulged, twisted and re-formed around it, the face above her didn't change. Didn't move, except for the tentacles reaching for her. Beckoning her to come a little closer, a little higher, so their hooked ends could snatch her up into the beak mouth.

"Sorry?" said the taxi driver.

She hadn't realised she had spoken. She had just been thinking it didn't look so much like a face in the clouds, as the face of something that lived above them. So immense that ordinarily she could never have seen it.

The face of something she ought never to have seen.

"I hope you left plenty early. We're here for however long this is gonna take," said the driver, waving at the queue of red rear-lights in front of him.

"Plenty of time," she said. Plenty of time for the storm to blow over, for the face she couldn't un-see to disperse. She closed her eyes and concentrated on her breathing.

By the time she made it to the airport, her plane was already boarding. The weather had unleashed a shower rather than a storm, and she had to hurry to her gate. It was easy to put the weird face she had imagined in the clouds out of her mind as she hurried through security. She was breathless as she joined the last stragglers lining up to board and found herself thinking of Reinhold as she waited to show her boarding pass.

Even at the end, when he'd been so agitated, he hadn't wanted to attack her. Not even after she'd maced him. He had wanted to keep her safe. Maybe it was true that he had only been defending himself on flight J620, when people panicked. Being big wasn't always an advantage. When there was a fight, people automatically assumed the bigger guy started it.

"Ma'am?" The steward smiled with thin fake patience, waiting for Dr Lorenz to hand over her pass to be scanned through.

Through the window the clouds had lightened, but she could still see a face in them. It was faint, but the hollows of the eye sockets were visible. The swirling cloud gave away the tentacles, and a single curved line under them formed a beak large enough to bite through the Boeing 747 she was due to fly on.

She took a step back. If she was seeing faces everywhere, it meant she was working too hard. It wouldn't help to go to a conference and have to admit that she was seeing faces everywhere herself. She needed a break. Urgently.

———

She half expected to find the same taxi driver waiting for her outside. That's how it would happen in a movie, but she got a different one.

It was the same traffic jam, though. She started counting the stranded taxis around them for something to do, to avoid looking up in case the face pushing down through the clouds was still there. If it was, she wanted to leave it at the airport.

"You believe this traffic?" asked the taxi driver, the way they all did, and her spirits lifted. It was good to be home.

"Unbelievable," she agreed, happily resting her head against the petrified leather of the headrest. The car inched forward and stopped again. She'd have to go grocery shopping, now that she wasn't going to Boston, but there was yoghurt and cereal, and coffee in the flat. It could wait until tomorrow.

A flash in the sky caught her attention.

"Christ!" The driver was craning over the steering wheel to see a ballooning explosion. A moment later, the roar of it, the cracking of the plane's body as it split in two, reached them. They watched in horror as the fading daylight glinted off the metal body of an airplane tumbling out of the sky.

Page One

My goals for this flash fiction were to write (a) a Choose Your Own Adventure style story, and (b) the most depressing thing I could think of.
Yes, it's short, but there's no limit to how often you can play.
Enjoy!

———

You are your country's greatest surgeon. But as the sun rises over the bullet-scarred city, the hospital has two patients waiting for a heart transplant, and only a single heart available.

One patient is the beloved, ageing musician, whose powerful music has helped your country's army through the civil war. He arrived yesterday.

The other patient is a young girl. She has done nothing for her country, but has been waiting for months.

To heal the beloved musician, turn to page 4.
To heal the girl, turn to page 7.

———

You chose to heal the girl.

Then the phone rang.

Your president sounds exactly like he does on the radio.

You force yourself to answer. Like everyone, you are used to saying nothing when the president speaks. The cafes are never as silent as when the president talks on the radio. He says he is a brave man, who made many sacrifices to lead your country through the recent troubles. Why should he not request the occasional favour?

The musician is a personal friend of the president, and the country needs his music. The girl is just a girl.

That phone call makes your mind up.

You affix your signature to a chart and send it to the hospital's administrators.

If you changed your mind and signed the form to operate on the musician, turn to page 12.

If you chose to be brave like your president, and stand by your decision to help the girl, turn to page 16.

———

You chose to be brave. Your country needs a future, and can choose its own music.

The phone rings again.

The general is also a close friend of the musician. His men have fought so hard, and need music for their celebratory parades.

You wonder who from the hospital's administration denounced you. You knew you would be caught, but had hoped to gain enough time to save the girl.

The general praises your wife and two boys. They have made him feel at home in your apartment. He is happy to wait with them until you can confirm the patient is on the mend.

If you decide to take his words at face value, turn to page 22.

If you heed the implied threat, turn to page 26.

———

You protected your family. Of course you did.

Besides, now the choice is between saving *four* lives or *one*.

Maybe even *five* lives, if they need your obedience more than your skill.

The musician's body is pale and flaccid on the table. His vital signs remain regular and slow—*adagissimo*—throughout the operation. Easy.

You dispatch a porter on a bicycle to inform the general that the operation on his friend was successful.

If you wait behind the door to ambush the general when he comes to see his friend—time for him to make a sacrifice—turn to page 35.

If you get back to work, as if nothing has happened, turn to page 33.

You continue working at the hospital as usual.

Why not? You are your country's greatest surgeon.

Is it too far-fetched to think your president may one day require your skill for himself?

If you think it is too far-fetched to believe that next time things will be different, you can stop reading. Well done!

If you think it is not too far-fetched, turn to the start of PAGE ONE and start again.

Blackpriest

The fictional town of Tullamore in this uncanny tale of supernatural forces has nothing to do with the town of Tullamore that I grew up in, okay?
Having said that, I always loved the King Oak at Charleville Castle, and there's Tullamore Dew whiskey.
So there's that.

———

I felt all kinds of awful at Tadhg's funeral, although the grief hadn't hit me yet. The call had been too surprising, and the numbing sense of unreality hadn't yet faded. Watching the coffin ease into the boggy earth made it worse.

I felt like an imposter for being there at all, as I hadn't seen him in years. Tadhg and I had been best friends growing up, but we hadn't kept in touch.

Mostly, though, I felt fury that only five people stood around the grave, including the priest, who read from his book on one side of the gaping earth.

I had brought my mother, and we stood on the other side with Tadhg's parents, Mr and Mrs Matthews.

Neither Tadhg nor I had ever been popular. I still wasn't, and, after several years working in Galway, I still only knew a bare handful of people from work to go for a drink with, but Tadhg had spent his whole life in Tullamore. There should have been more people. It was a small town and close-knit.

One girl I'd briefly dated at University had said the town still "clung" to me before we broke up.

I was angriest at the tiny Mrs Matthews. It should have been her funeral. But in the October sun, she looked healthy, though as fragile as ever. She'd always been sick. Fine lines intricately scored her face, like it had been expertly cracked over and over again, like a well-worn china plate held together only by its glaze. She'd touched rather than shaken my hand when we arrived at the funeral.

Mr Matthews had given me his usual confused, appraising stare when I offered my condolences, and sweat pricked through my shirt. I remembered his awkward pauses from visiting Tadhg. When I was younger, I'd had a secret crush on his wife, and was always terrified in case the look meant he had somehow worked it out, and that one day he'd tell on me.

My own mother was fading fast, but insisted she was fine to go to the hotel afterwards. We sat together in an empty room in front of cold sandwiches and glazed lemon cakes. After my mother had picked among several of them, she angrily announced she was cold, as if we had arranged it all on purpose to annoy her, and we left. On the way out, Mrs Matthews asked me to call around the next day to do her a favour. I promised I would, barely daring to breathe in case she finally fell apart in front of me.

At home, the phone was ringing from the hall as we got out of the car. I let us in with the key I'd had made twenty years ago.

"Can't you get that?" called my mother, who had gone straight into the kitchen, and the ringing stopped. "Mrs Matthews looked well," she said, when I joined her. She still hadn't said "How are you?" or "How long will you stay?" as though I'd never left.

I helped her get her gloves off and she went out to the garden without changing the rest of her clothes. The bed in the spare room was damp from disuse, but I found my old sleeping bag in the airing cupboard. That would do.

I dreamt of the blackpriest for the first time in years that night. He stood in the garden, looking up at the bedroom window. I woke before a pale, waterlogged figure joined him from the shadows. It couldn't have been Tadhg, because Tadhg hadn't drowned.

He'd blown his brains out with his father's shotgun.

————

"Can't you stop it ringing?" Mrs Matthews' voice was so faint when she spoke, that it was absurd she should outlive her own son. She pushed the brick of an old GPS device, covered in black and orange rubber, over the table towards me. The LCD display dimmed as she spoke. It was Tadhg's, back from when we used to go geocaching. His parents had got it for him for Christmas. I had nothing like it, so I had volunteered my weekly pocket money to be used for "swag," items to trade for the contents of the caches.

Tadhg had loved being out in nature.

But I think, even back then, I was only looking for a way out of the place.

"It's been ringing for days now, and I can't turn it off." She gave me an encouraging smile, as if to say I should answer it right now.

"It's his GPS," I said. Did she think it was a phone?

"You'll know what to do with it, though," she said.

Mr Matthews, who'd been hanging around in the hallway, saw me to the door. "GPS, is it?"

"Tadhg's. I'll see if I can stop it beeping." Had Tadhg still been geocaching before he died? Or had his mother switched it on while going through his things?

Mr Matthews didn't respond. His gaze travelled all over me. I could smell his breakfast on him. Eggs, and toast, and instant coffee. As always, anything I said took ages to get through to him. "Right," he said at last. "Your Mammy's well?"

I tried to decide between a comfortable but childish "My Mammy's fine" or a grown-up but awkward "My mother, Heather? As well as can be expected, thank you." He took a step towards me and I said, "Yes, Mr Matthews." He reached over my shoulder to undo the top lock on the door, trapping me in the corridor.

"You're a good lad," he said. He shook my hand, too hard, and his face was grey, like the stones he made his money with. I searched his face for something to remind me of Tadhg, but there was nothing I recognised anymore. For all the resemblance between them, he could just as easily have been my dad.

Growing up, I had never known my own father and had liked it when people confused me and Tadhg for brothers, but without him there to connect us, it just felt wrong.

A burst of song from the kitchen shattered the silence of the dull hallway. Mrs Matthews was singing. I had always assumed they were religious songs, though I could never make out any words, and the singing, full of high, tumbling grace notes, sounded more like a trapped bird's desperate call than anything I'd ever heard in a church.

Mr Matthews moved away from me. "And you're all right?"

"Yes."

The GPS beeped at me on the way home. In the front garden my mother tugged at a clump of dock leaves in the flowerbed, with her feet resting in a patch of oil in the grass. I'd check the lawnmower when I got a chance. The GPS beeped again as I passed her to go inside.

"Will you not get that?" she asked. A large black bin bag lurked behind her, with only a handful of leaves and grass stalks in it: her entire morning's work. I left her to it and went in to cook lunch with the last of the potatoes in the house, with frozen burgers from the local shop.

"I'm going shopping. I'll be back late," I said.

She nodded, but was watching the news when I walked into the rain. I stayed for a few pints, and the night had settled around the town before I started back.

Knots of people had clotted outside pub doorways, where they'd been banished to smoke. They glared at me as I passed, but it meant nothing. It was just Midlands hospitality. Through bright fast-food restaurant windows, teenagers tore into greasy burgers to feed their acne. Once I'd left the few streets that made up the town centre, solitary cars buzzed on the hazy, empty roads. Few of them bothered to dip their lights as they approached, leaving me dazzled and blind every time they passed. The drizzle dampened my footsteps and hissed on the road with a low static buzz.

I noticed a figure in the distance ahead of me. Thumbing a lift, I thought, but it kept pace with me. Perhaps it was a neighbour then, someone's squat granny in her housecoat, looking for me to deliver more bad news: my mother had taken a bad turn. I started to hurry to catch up until the beer washed up an old memory. The blackpriest in his bat-wing cassock.

Originally, the blackpriest had been Tadhg's nightmare. I learned about him the first time we visited Charleville Castle for a paper-chase, when we were ten years old. I suppose it must have been someone's birthday, though I don't know who would have invited us. Or perhaps the volunteers who worked there had organised it to raise money for the castle's restoration. At any rate, I remember climbing the enormous and ancient King Oak at the entrance to the grounds, waiting for the game to begin. I teamed up with Tadhg, of course. He'd brought a compass, and I was good at school, so I was sure we'd win.

Everyone split up to hunt the paper clues, and we cut through the woods so no one could follow us. We found the first bit of paper easily, then Tadhg said a man had the next piece. He had held it up under his chin for us to see it, before turning and running, so we hared after him, thinking the game was brilliant. It wasn't until we had left the grounds of Charleville Estate, and stranded ourselves in a waste of wide, barren fields separated by nondescript trees, that we worried something might be wrong. We wandered for hours, trying to find our way back as the day grew colder and the shadows lengthened. I kept saying, "If we just go in a straight line, then we'll have to get to a road. We can work it out from there."

But we didn't get to a road. Instead, we found ourselves in the ruins of a monastery set amongst overgrown gardens, the grass up to our waists. Moss softened the old walls, and birds called harsh questions through the broken windows to scare us off.

"There he is," said Tadhg. It was already evening, and I only saw a shadow in the ruins. We knew not to go into a strange house after a strange man in the middle of nowhere. There were no houses nearby, and there'd be no help for us if he was a pervert.

"Come on." I hurried around to the front of the house instead, Tadhg watching the monastery behind us, while I wondered how we'd got there in the first place. I was sure the monastery was on the far side of town, with the river in the way.

The monastery was an historic site, so the owners of the land were required by law to let people in, but that didn't mean they had to like it, and a thick length of chain was wrapped around the entrance gates to make it looked locked and discourage visitors. In the cold, my hands struggled to untangle them.

"It's the blackpriest," said Tadhg. I could barely hear him over a low groaning noise which gathered behind us. The sound filled my ears and wrapped itself around my brain as I imagined a priest crying and bellowing as he raced to catch us. I panicked before the chain clattered off the gates. I pulled Tadhg through behind me without even looking back.

A blue Datsun was speeding towards Kilbeggan as we spilled onto the road. It was Mr Matthews out looking for us. His car smelled of fried fish, cut grass and machine oil when we got in. He took us home in silence. We didn't pass Charleville on the way.

After that, we made sure to avoid any cache coordinates set near the monastery. A little later, Tadhg told me he was going to be a priest, although he didn't sound happy about it.

I'd always assumed we were both equally desperate to get out of town, but with his mother always so sick, perhaps he knew he'd have to stay.

———

The figure on the road ahead of me disappeared into the darkness beyond the furthest streetlight. Tadhg lived—used to live—further down that road. I was glad to have the street to myself again, though I couldn't shake the feeling that the figure had walked backwards into the dark, so I'd be sure to see the white collar under its chin.

The electric burr of the streetlights and hissing of the drizzle faded to nothingness as I continued walking. I coughed to disturb the claustrophobic silence. It came out muffled, and the hairs on the back of my neck rose when it was answered by something in the dark ahead of me. I'd only heard that noise once before, but had never forgotten it. It vibrated through my shoes and wound its way up my legs, coil by throbbing, nauseating coil, until, by the time it reached my ears, it caused them to ache. A low groan of anguish, rushing towards me with the violence of a hurricane from where the dark figure had disappeared.

From out of the dark beyond the last streetlight: more darkness. The edges of the blacker darkness flickered and snapped, sucking up the orange glow of the sodium streetlights, pulling all light into itself.

A huge, winged creature as black as the space between stars sped towards me. Atop the figure was the blackpriest's face. Nicotine-yellowed skin was pulled taut over cheekbones, stretched between enormous black eyes and wide open mouth. His cassock flapped around him, stretching over the road on one side and into the hedges on the other. He flew over the ground, close enough for his hovering feet to merge into his own shadow. In seconds he had arrived at the second streetlight, his oily hair gleaming. As he passed under the streetlights, his shadow toyed with me, zipping ahead first to bite me, before allowing the groaning blackpriest's gravity to pull it back on its leash.

Only three streetlights separated us and I couldn't move, watching him grow and grow. Some kink in perspective allowed him to grow two or three times faster than he should have as he screamed towards me. By the next streetlight, his head hung high above me and his feet and legs hung far below the surface of the road. Behind him, the world had become a gaping void. Once he reached me, I'd fall into it and be lost. And I couldn't move.

The scream of his agony was a solid wall of noise trapping me in place. I wanted to close my eyes, hide in the darkness of my own head, but he wouldn't let me escape that way. He—it—stared straight at me, hungry and furious that I'd evaded him so long. In another second, I'd disappear into the black hole of his cassock. The pocked, dried skin of his face cracked as he opened his eyes and mouth wider until it ripped and they formed one cold, bitter-stinking abyss.

"Hop in," said a voice behind me.

The words didn't register until the man said them again.

"Hop in."

I must have closed my eyes after all. I turned to see Mr Matthews in his car, the window wound down.

"Hi." It was all I could manage as I got in. I felt lightheaded in the new silence. Mr Matthews' hand brushed my leg as he changed gears when we reached my house.

"You're a good lad," he said.

"I wish there was something I could have done," I said.

His car drove off after I had closed the front door of my mother's house behind me. Loud religious music from the telly, or the radio, or somewhere saturated the hallway. It cut out as I entered the kitchen, where my mother sat under a rug in front of the dead television.

The GPS woke me several times during the night, rescuing me from dreams of someone waiting outside in the rain.

"I'm going for a walk," I told my mother's back the next day, as she tugged at something in the flower bed. I had Tadhg's GPS in my rucksack.

———

My mother had moved to Tullamore for work when I was still a baby. She had always hated it, but it was all I knew.

I hated it, too.

We almost never arrived. Back when she still used to talk, she'd often tell me the story. How, after she had packed our last belongings into our old car, I'd bawled my head off, when Mr Brown, my favourite teddy bear, was missing. There'd been a big fight when my mother said she was leaving, and after her big exit, she had to go back for Mr Brown, and the whole thing kicked off again.

It wasn't until after dark that she was finally able to start driving. Even now, the country roads are narrow and winding. And back then, before the money from the European Union started to flow, they were also pot-holed all to hell. On the outskirts of the town, a truck carrying sacks of agricultural fertiliser almost crushed us as it sped around a corner. The narrowness of the road saved it from jack-knifing. Instead, it had catapulted its load at us, dozens of fifty kilo sacks, destroying the engine, frosting the windshield, but leaving us alive.

For weeks afterwards, my mother found the tiny round orange pellets in the car, and a trail of them followed us wherever we drove. "But we made it," she always finished, her lips turned down with deep disappointment.

I followed the GPS's coordinates to Charleville Estate. The cache was in a fork on one of the lower branches of the ancient King Oak. I remembered it.

It was where Tadhg and I had waited to play paper-chase. The cache was the small plastic case for a roll of 35 mm film. Inside was the logbook, and a plastic soldier. The soldier sighted along a rifle with a barrel so bent that if he were to shoot, the bullet would circle around and hit him in the back of the head.

The logbook contained less than a page of "logs," people listing their User-ID to prove they'd found it. I recognised our old tag, but didn't add anything this time. The GPS beeped. On the way here, I'd stopped outside a newsagent for swag to trade. The newsagent had one of those machines where you insert a coin and twist a handle to release a plastic egg. The egg was too big for the cache, so I popped it open. There was a small blue toy car inside. I swapped the car for the soldier and continued on.

The coordinates took me past Charleville Castle where, at this time of year, the ground was soggy and treacherous with leaves. The trunk of a storm-felled tree had a cheap Tupperware-style box tucked inside it. I ignored the logbook and examined the swag, a tarnished silver locket, without a photo. It belonged to Mr Matthews.

Mrs Matthews had given it to him when they were dating. There had been a photo in it when Tadhg had shown it to me: his mother with an outdated hairstyle, but otherwise looking exactly the same as she always had. It had been at the height of my crush on her, and I had stolen it twice.

Each time, I sneaked back to replace it, before I ever left their house.

In exchange for it now, I left the plastic egg from the newsagent's machine filled with round orange fertiliser pellets from the garden shed at home.

The GPS beeped again, but I didn't need it. All I had to do was keep going straight, and I'd get there.

Both of us should have been living our own lives by now. I should have a wife and kids. As a priest, Tadhg should have his faith and a happy flock of parishioners. We should be catching up over occasional drinks. Instead, Tadhg was in the ground, and I had a job in Galway and a small flat, both of which seemed more unreal the longer I stayed here.

The plan had been for us to go to Maynooth, because Tadhg could study to be a priest there while I studied Arts. Towards the end of our second last year in school, Tadhg's mother got sick, or sick-*er*. He missed loads of school to look after her and help his father with housework. At first I went to visit, but he was always sulking and looking for a fight. When I didn't visit, he sulked and the next time he saw me in school, demanded to know why I didn't come around. It had been a terrible year for him, but I had hated it, too. So when he failed his exams, and I got the letter accepting me to Maynooth, I didn't think twice. I didn't break off our friendship.

I just left. His mother was on the mend, and I'd got out of the habit of dealing with his father.

Tadhg's father had always stared at me as if he couldn't believe I was real, and when I stopped visiting Tadhg, any sense of guilt I felt was outweighed by relief that I no longer had to suffer through the interminable pauses of his conversation, the awkwardness of which had always made me break out in a sweat.

———

"Done your homework, have you?"

"Yes, Mr Matthews. There wasn't much today." I only ever met him in the narrow hallway on the way to Tadhg's room.

His glasses travelled over my face, as if looking for a clue how to translate what I'd just said. "Ah, good. Good. And your Mammy's well?"

"Fine, thanks." I waited for that information to be processed. Then he noticed with surprise that I was wearing a school uniform, and his eyes travelled all over it, while sweat dribbled down my sides from my prickling armpits.

"Lovely. And you're alright, are you?"

"Yes, Mr Matthews."

The brass clock hanging inside the kitchen tocked slowly through the open door. I counted eight tocks. Always the same questions, always the same answers.

Nine tocks.

Ten.

"Well, I won't keep you," he'd say, and I could go. Tadhg's parents were great believers in "fresh air," so Tadhg's bedroom was always cold from the open window, and the first gulp of it tasted sweet after talking to Mr Matthews.

Tadhg said his father was religious, as if that explained it.

I think it explained why Tadhg wanted to become a priest. Their back garden looked out onto the Grand Canal, and Mr Matthews often stood there fishing, his head shaking and twisting as if engaged in a discussion, or defending himself from accusations.

I knew the Matthews had made their money with stone, though I never knew exactly how. I assumed they had a quarry, but Mr Matthews was always hanging around the house or else fishing when I was there. Sometimes I wondered, or perhaps I should say wished, that Mr Matthews was hanging around to find the opportunity to tell me something important, but any time it looked like our "conversation" would go beyond the usual call and response, Mrs Matthews would startle us by breaking into intense, warbling song. When I mentioned it once, Tadhg told me his mother never sang, so maybe she was religious too, and it was a prayer.

Bits of farm equipment had been left in the shed out the back when they'd bought their house. A ruined plough with bent and jagged blades, an old tractor, originally red, now brown with rust. We called it "the Massive Ferguson," because of the oversized back wheels. Tadhg sat on it one day and told me he'd been dreaming about the blackpriest.

The blackpriest waited in the garden for Tadhg to come out. When I told him it was just a dream, he showed me a patch of grass with a black stain on it.

"That's where the blackpriest stands," he said.

It could have been oil, but it didn't make sense. "Why would you go out to some creepy priest?"

"Because otherwise he'll come in."

That, at least, made sense. I wouldn't want a creepy priest dripping oil in my house, either. "What happens when you go out?" I asked.

That's when Tadhg told me his mother was getting worse, and he had to help look after her.

———

I did my best to follow the route Tadhg and I had taken back then, but it was impossible. Even if things didn't seem to have changed much, it was a long time ago. I even tried getting deliberately lost, but the GPS told me I was still wrong.

After several hours of wandering, I realised I'd have to turn my phone to airplane mode. I'd kept the online maps open as a cheat. The countryside immediately felt different after that, and I started walking, as the sun eased itself towards the horizon. Night soon swept the last of the light out of the sky, so it was impossible to see whether I crossed the Tullamore River to get to the monastery. It didn't matter, just one more cache to go and it would all be over. The fields were damp, and the mud squished under my feet. Animals rattled through the surrounding undergrowth, and the air smelled of tobacco. The dark pressed against my face, tightened around my limbs.

When the GPS beeped, I dug my phone out of my pocket to use its flashlight. It shone on the mossy walls of the monastery. Tadhg must have come back here alone at some point. We had never gone this close to it. The GPS beeped again, and I searched the base of the wall, stinging my hands on nettles.

The wind rose and flustered the long grass, which whipped my legs. I followed the wall around until I heard the hollow thump of a plank. I lifted it, the wood slimy with rain, and insects scattered from a hole, in which a ten-litre tub of house paint squatted. Inside that was a five-litre metal paint can, liver-spotted with rust. I pried the lid off with a coin.

The swag was a single shotgun cartridge wrapped in tissue and plastic. I swapped my watch for it.

The sense of being watched came back and increased as I moved away from the shelter of the wall into the view of the empty windows. The wind groaned with a low, pained roar, warning me the blackpriest was coming. Stone squealed and screeched as it moved. I wished I could turn off my flashlight, which exposed my position in the darkness, but I needed it to get out of here. The groaning was louder than ever and my neck burned in anticipation of the blackpriest grabbing it. Grass swished and trees bent and the monastery itself shifted in the dark behind me.

I ran and made it to the gates, tangled shut with the heavy chain. My hands trembled as I fumbled with the knot. The groan was a physical force behind me. The screeching of stone on stone pierced my ears. Something enormous was coming for me, crawling out of the ground, out of hell, to get me. The gates were slick with rain when I tried climbing them, but with the chain's knot as a foothold, I got one hand over the top before the weight of my rucksack pulled me back. My skull cracked on the gravel path. The flashlight winked out, but light shone from somewhere.

Behind me, the monastery was closer than it should have been. Its massive double doors were the blackpriest's mouth, the windows were his eyes. He swam through the overgrown grass, just the blackpriest's enormous head visible, the rest of him hidden underground. He opened his mouth and the building's foundations screamed as he pulled it through the soil like a whale after plankton to catch me in his mouth, to tumble me into the dark of his basement. His head kept growing, the walls of the monastery bulging, until the moss of the blackpriest's gangrenous granite skin blocked out everything, as the walls cracked around his mouth.

I staggered to my feet and slammed bodily into the gates, screaming for help. The chains clinked, then unravelled and dropped to the ground. I burst into the road, and a battered blue Datsun almost ran me over. Mr Matthews wordlessly pushed open the passenger door and took me home.

I found a bottle of whiskey in the cupboard.

Eventually I slept, and the blackpriest was in my garden. It wasn't a nightmare, though, it was an ending.

My mother was there, too. Still confused and bitter, but more like her old self.

Tadhg was there, and he looked pleased to see me.

Mr and Mrs Matthews were there. Mrs Matthews singing, Mr Matthews waiting.

I dressed and made my way to the front door. A floorboard creaked and from its bed the body of my mother yelled, "Get that, will you?" as if whatever she'd spent so long waiting for had finally arrived. The bite of the night air brought the blood to my cheeks as I made my way to Tadhg's house.

My prizes: the locket; the soldier; and the shotgun cartridge were in my pocket. The GPS hung from my belt. When I arrived, I didn't know what to do. Tadhg was dead and his parents were asleep.

I crunched through their property to the Grand Canal at the back, which flows to the River Shannon, and where Mr Matthews fished. Once it had carried tonnes of freight, these days only the occasional houseboat of German tourists floated by, and the surface was motionless.

I stopped at the worn patch in the grass where Mr Matthews always stood and peered into the water. Something glimmered in the depths, a fish-belly white form: Tadhg.

Pike had eaten his eyes, leaving black water-filled holes as he stared up at me. His fingers and arms were too long, melted and attenuated from the water. But strong. He reached out and grabbed my feet. The cold of his grasp was shocking, and I stumbled backwards, pulling him out of the water with me. When he stood, he towered over me. Water rushed out of his distended mouth and splashed over my head. It ran into my mouth to steal my breath.

Behind me, Mrs Matthews started singing. When I turned, Mr Matthews offered me the shotgun. The blackpriest hovered behind them, his hands joined in prayer. Tadhg's hand was freezing on my shoulder as he brought me to the group. His mother looked young and pretty in the moonlight, but Mr Matthews hugged me too tightly, pressing his full body against mine.

"Thank you," he said.

I couldn't remember what the last thing I'd said to him was.

I stood on a smear of oil that mirrored the endless night sky. Mr Matthews showed me how to load the shotgun. It embarrassed me that I didn't know how to do it myself. But it's the kind of thing a boy learns from his father, and I'd never known mine. Still, I felt like I'd ruined the moment.

I should have used my time in Galway to have a family of my own, so my son would know what to do when it was his turn.

I hoped Tadhg wouldn't make the same mistake once he finally got out of here.

The blackpriest faced the four of us and groaned as he fed on the light from the moon and stars. It poured into him, swelling his shadow until there was no dark other than that of the blackpriest. Mrs Matthews trilled her gibberish song in praise, as Mr Matthews helped me position my hands on the gun.

When he clapped me on the shoulder, I knew it was time. I squeezed the trigger and my body tumbled into the dark.

Beauty is skin deep.
Cut deeper.

People Skins, Volume 0: Hidden Cuts features 5 more tales of off-beat fantasy and surreal horror—but only for subscribers: a sheriff finds ice-cold dread in the middle of a red-hot desert; Ireland's miracle of moving religious statues becomes a nightmare; Rose, Henry, and Reg are friends, lovers, and playing a deadly game; Maria doesn't believe a ghost haunts the phone box. But she will; a fugitive pirate ship encounters a wreck with a mind of its own.

Join me to get your *Hidden Cuts now!*
(https://morgandelaney.info/newsletter/)

Acknowledgments

Thanks, as ever, to Nadine, who makes it possible for me to write, and is there for me when I stumble bleary-eyed and confused away from my computer. I love you, mwah!

Thanks to Siggi, Renate, and Petra and Uwe Weidemann for everything.

Thanks to Julian Barr for editing these stories and also showing me how paragraphs work (it's all very technical, I won't bore you with the details).

And thanks to everyone who read this book or its individual stories in all their various forms.

If you enjoyed this book, please leave a great review, which is the best marketing a book can get.

Several of these stories appeared first in my newsletter. If you want stories and more, sign up at: https://morgandelaney.info/newsletter/

About the Author

Morgan Delaney is an Irish writer of dark and fantastic fiction. Like the great Irish writers, Morgan prefers to live abroad. "The place is shaped like a teddy bear, but they called it the Celtic *Tiger*. You don't really know where you are," he explains.

He has lived in Ireland, Germany, Australia, Kazakhstan and Georgia, and worked, among other things, as a building engineer, until one day, while he was writing a particularly outrageous cost estimate, the wind changed.

And he has been stuck like that—writing lies—ever since.

His favourite film is Terry Gilliam's Brazil.

Also By Morgan Delaney

Light reading

The Alumière Sisters' Adventures
The Devil Rode Out (a subscriber exclusive)
The Phoenix
The Squared Circle (coming soon!)

Darker and stranger

People Skins. Dark, Strange and Fantastic Stories
People Skins, Volume 0: Hidden Cuts (a subscriber exclusive)
People Skins, Volume 1
People Skins, Volume 2

Pure Horror

Short, Sharp Horror Shocks
Sour Milk
Quick Deaths

www.ingramcontent.com/pod-product-compliance
Lightning Source LLC
LaVergne TN
LVHW091304190726
843491LV00001B/406